RUINS OF THE IMMORTAL

Elijah T Landers

Landers Publishing

CONTENTS

CHAPTER ONE: DOCTOR

Few records remain of the ancients in the time before the collapse. Rumors circulate on their fate, and the mystery drives scholars and adventurers mad. The lingering legacy of those ancients is a burning question of what caused their demise. A legacy that curses the mind of a certain wanderer that roams across the land.

The gargantuan ruins of a domed city once called the jewel of the galaxy, the object of fascination by scholars and treasure hunters. Near this site, a youth, recently knighted, roams with a question lingering in his mind. The armor of the youth sparkles with a new polish. The belts and straps were recently replaced, his boots barely dirty, and a stainless surcoat with a large golden sun in a sharp and simplistic design.

This is not his first expedition to this vast landscape. Many times, he has gone roaming these same farmlands. The landscape and nature of the land barely changing in all the time he has wandered. Each trip, looking for a way inside. After unsuccessfully attempting to scale or find an opening in the walls, little hope remains for what he will find.

The knight lifts his visor and raises a handkerchief to his mouth. An old, abandoned mine, rudely constructed and opening into a deep cavern, lies before him. In the air, a stench of rot lingers. Pieces of abandoned cloth and old trash litter the cave ground. Deeper in the cave is more filth with the addition of a lone broken clock. He calls out, but no answer returns.

Coming to the deepest reaches of the cave. The smell gets more putrid as the remains of some unlucky thief sit against the wall. Curses and eventually words escape the knight's coughing, "What would drive someone to dwell in such a place?"

From the corner of his eye comes a light and the sound of footsteps from behind. He slides his greatsword off his shoulder and unsheathes his blade. Lowering his visor and taking a defensive stance, he prepares for what may be robbers or some other unsavory folk who were forced to take shelter in this awful place. To his surprise, those who enter the room are not at all the people he expected. The first person he sees is a sick young man, not much older than a child, with red hair, pointed ears, two stubs on his forehead that are likely horns, and organic-looking red tattoos that make patterns on his face and body. His body is shaking, and he looks hesitant but gestures for someone else to come into the doorway. The next person he sees is a visibly pregnant woman, sweaty and sickly looking of the same race.

The knight, rightfully confused, questions the pair, "I can tell just by looking at you both that you should not have come down here. What demon possessed you to drag yourselves here?"

The man notices his wife struggling to walk, lifts her arm, and supports her. He meekly inquires, "You visited our village yesterday; you are a doctor, right?"

"No, I am not a doctor." His voice is cold. He gives a gesture to the couple as if to point out what he is wearing and the weapon he is holding.

"But you heal people, yes?"

Taritie lets out a long sigh. Knowing the couple is unlikely to have a hidden blade, he sheathes his sword. With a slick motion, he slings the sheathe onto his shoulder.

The man drops to his knees, "Please, sir, you do not have to heal me, but save my wife. She is pregnant, and if you do nothing, we will lose the baby."

"Have you not brought her to a real doctor?"

"They have all turned us away. We have no money."

"Why do you think I am different?" The knight takes one last look around. Examining the wall where a corpse lay. Reaching out his hand and feeling the stone.

"You healed a man in my village and asked him for

nothing in return. The moment I heard, I chased after you with my wife."

"You would bring your wife and follow me into the depths of a dark mine? You could have run into any number of fiends, monsters, bandits, or even trapped by a cave-in down here. Do you have no common sense?"

"The sickness that we have has already killed my father and brother. We are already the dead walking."

"Curse your persistence! Fine, you and your wife sit down. I will take a look at you."

The knight takes off his sword once more and places it against the wall. He removes his helmet, and the Feylin couple looks at him with surprise. Despite their preconceptions, the man is rather young-looking. His golden eyes are serious, and his brow reveals he is both tired and pained. His dark brown hair distinguishes him; he is certainly not a local Selestia or Feylin. His face looks humanoid, with somewhat pointed ears, and a slight glimmer of large canines appears while he talks. He has no energy veins that can be seen on his pale, sun-tanned face; he does have what looks to be black markings with golden dust that do not seem to be painted and look almost natural. The knight proceeds to remove his gauntlets, revealing large, fearsome-looking hands. He goes over to feel the man and then the woman's head. He signals for them to open their mouths, and after inspection, he grabs their wrists and applies pressure.

The woman, with a quivering voice, asks the knight as he is checking her pulse, "Where did you learn how to heal? The man in the village you healed had been suffering from that disease for months. No doctor could treat him."

The knight mutters under his breath a complaint, clears his throat, and answers, "Please! if the doctors knew anything, they would have discovered he was merely suffering from stomach issues caused by the water. I only treated his symptoms, then advised him to change wells or drink more wine."

"Was that all?"

"Believe me, when I told him to merely drink more wine, I have never seen a wider smile."

"What is your name?"

"I am called Taritie. If you are wondering where the name is from, it is the language of the Shappalans." Taritie grabs from his pouch a journal and looks through it. He asks, "What is your name, by the way?"

The man answers, "I am Tyrnol, and my wife is Myriusha."

"If I had known how interesting your names were, I probably would not have tried to defend my own name." Taritie takes a moment before apologizing, "Sorry, I am not calling your names weird; it is just… never mind.”

"You do not need to apologize; many of the people in this area do not like us or our names. The locals are mostly those who have the blood of Selestia. They do not like my kin.”

Taritie finds a few things written in his journal that are similar to their symptoms. Before he says anything for certain, he asks, "When did this start? Do you remember what may have led to this?”

Tyrnol is about to speak but is interrupted by Myriusha, who spits, "I know what caused this! The merchant that sells Kleblau fruit started setting aside underripe bushels just for us. It was not long later my husband's father died. He poisoned us, I know it!”

Tyrnol soothes her. "The fruit was underripe, and yes, he is a vile man, yet I do not think he was poisoning us.”

"Actually, what she is saying makes sense. He may not have been intentionally poisoning you. However, many fruits could cause your symptoms. What was the name of that fruit again?”

Myriusha says, "My husband's father always enjoyed these small blue fruits called Kleblau fruit. They were his favorite, and I would even sneak a few into our meals sometime.”

"Unfortunately, there is little I can do. For starters, it was a mistake coming down here, both of you need plenty of fresh air, water, and it is best to eat plenty of bread."

Myriusha's cheeks turn red, and with fire in her tone, "What do you mean, is that all you can recommend? This killed my stepfather and stepbrother, and all you can tell us is to get air, drink water, and eat what we have already been eating?"

"You should also stay away from alcohol."

Tyrnol interrupts her from starting to scream and says to Taritie, "Thank you for your help, I will follow your advice as best as I can." Myriusha begins to sob. Tyrnol comforts her, helping her to her feet. With sunken expressions, they turn away.

Taritie bites his lip, before gathering his things and following after them. He walks alongside them, raising Myriusha's arm and supporting her as she walks. The couple look in surprise at Taritie. "I can help you back to town, it is the least I can do."

Taritie thinks to himself that he has already thoroughly searched the mines. What he probably needs to do now is restock provisions; he may as well help them back to their home.

After helping them home, he finds himself caring for them. After they started to show signs of getting better, they convinced him to stay a couple more days. The first snow fell during that time, and the roads iced over. He helped them deliver their child and supported them through the worst of the winter.

Despite living outside the village and having no money, the family did not have a bad life. Myriusha was a talented cook and gatherer from a notable family in the north; they often sent her books and supplies. Tyrnol is talented with his hands. The house he built is both sturdy and cozy. The little house, positioned in the mountains outside the village, did not seem at all impoverished. In fact, Taritie finds himself wishing he could leave his work behind and stay here. To lean back in a chair and enjoy his days with friends. Despite this, an urge like an unscratchable itch lifts into his brain. He knows he has stayed too long. Now, it is time for him to return.

Taritie wakes early in the morning when the sun's rays peak over the horizon. He looks over at his two friends, Myriusha and Tyrnol, who have spent much of the night caring for their crying child. They fell asleep on a bench with the baby snuggled in Tyrnol's arms. The baby, unlike her parents, is not asleep. Wide awake, she wants to explore. The seed of curiosity inside her is fully awake, and she desires to move and crawl. Taritie, wanting to leave, turns away, and as he does, he hears a thud. He looks behind him to see the child sliding down Tyrnol and crawling after him.

Taritie groans in a whisper, "Ashanna what are you doing?" All that can be heard as a reply is senseless babbling as

Ashanna starts climbing him. The child has never seen Taritie in his armor. It fascinates her. She continues to play on his feet until Taritie picks her up, taking her out onto the porch, cradling her.

Taritie sits on a chair and takes pleasure in the scenery. He watches the sun rise above the mountains. He sees a fog hovering above the trees. Like a living creature, the smoke seems to move and ride along the mountain ridges with a mind of its own. Glistening snow can be seen below the fog. It has partially melted, and green patches are visible on the steep slopes. In front of the house, three deer wander into a clearing clustered with tree stumps. The deer do not notice or care about Taritie and baby Ashanna. They continue grazing and slowly move across the clearing. When the deer passes by and a rabbit darts out of sight, Taritie looks down to see Ashanna's smile and her hands bobbing up and down in excitement.

"I was worried about what kind of life a child would have under those two idiots; however, after living here for a while, I am not anymore. You have a wonderful life ahead of you." Ashanna did not care about Taritie's words; instead, she was entranced by the necklace around his neck.

The necklace is a simple steel chain with an extra link at the end connecting it to a small crest with two swords, wings, and a crown. "I am certain you will grow up to be strong here;

your mother can teach you how to read, and your father can teach you how to use your hands. You are truly blessed in this life."

Ashanna yanks on the chain. Taritie reels forward, followed by a groan. He grabs the necklace and, taking it off his head, hands it to her. The necklace is far too large for her little head and body; nonetheless, she is overjoyed to have it. She continues to babble and now starts to suck on the necklace as Taritie lets out a sigh, knowing that his mother's necklace is going to be mistreated in her hands.

Taritie hears subtle and tired footsteps approaching and looks to the door to see Myruisha. Getting up from his seat, he hands Ashanna to Myriusha. She gives a gentle smile at Taritie and lowers her head to give the same smile to Ashanna. In a tired voice, she says, "You are dressed and packed."

Taritie, answering the question she did not ask, says, "It is time I returned to duty. I have things left undone, and I could not live with myself if I simply abandoned them."

"I suppose I understand. I do not know how we can ever begin to repay you for your help."

"I knew from the start you could not repay me. Even still, you have cooked for me, given me lodging, and treated me as your own. That is payment enough."

"Your heart is purer than most I have known in this land.

If you do not mind me asking, what matter is so important it calls for your attention?"

"I swore to serve a kingdom in this land. That kingdom is in danger of war, and I would be embarrassed if I did not uphold my oath and fight for them."

"My father fought in a war, and even though he did not die, the man who returned was not the one I knew. Are you sure you would not rather stay with us?"

"I would much rather stay with you, but I was put on this earth for a purpose. I would be ashamed for all my days if I ran away."

"It seems this world has a way of throwing us into things we are not prepared for. Both of us are so young that people still call us children, and yet I am a mother, and you a soldier. Why is it that we cannot simply enjoy life as it comes?"

A cold wind blows from over the mountains and hits both of them, causing them to shiver. Taritie sees Ashanna shivering and knows neither of them has time for a lengthy discussion. "It would be no fun otherwise."

Despite his response, it is clear to Myriusha that Taritie is scared. It is not just the cold that is causing him to shiver as he walks out into the snow. Myriusha watches him from her porch until he disappears into the forest. Tyrnol comes behind her, wrapping her in a blanket and gently guiding her inside.

Ashanna, nothing more than a small child, is just beginning her adventure in life. A child born to a poor family, but nonetheless determined to survive in this world. She will surely face hardships and would not be granted the same playing field as those around her, yet what her future holds is entirely up to her.

The red-headed baby clutches the necklace given to her, memorizing every bit of the strange new object. Her amber eyes marvel at the little crown with crystals, even as the crown glows with an odd green hue. A voice, like a whisper, calls out to the necklace. Somewhere, machines begin to come to life, and old relics begin to reactivate. A certain man whose body has been frozen in a time long ago, takes a deep breath and disturbs the frost gathered on his clothes.

CHAPTER TWO: PEACE

"Ashanna, have you finished cleaning your room yet?" Myriusha calls from outside Ashanna's window. Myriusha weeds the outside vegetable garden. Thankfully for her, it was just outside of Ashanna's room, so she could check to see the progress of cleaning.

"Yes, Mother, see, does it not look great?" She gestures to her room. Myriusha pauses from weeding and pokes her head up and into the window. She spies an empty room but something about it does not sit right with her.

Grabbing the rim of the window, Myriusha leans inside, further scanning the room and inside her closet. She notices the nervous expression on Ashanna and knows something is going on.

Above Myriusha's head, clinging to the ceiling is where the dirt, trash, shoes, and clothes that Ashanna was supposed to have cleaned float. Using the power of her Feylin blood, energy pours out from the tips of her left hand hidden behind her back.

"I do not know how you are doing it, but I know that room is not clean. Are you certain that if I stop what I am doing and walk into your room, I will like what I see?"

Ashanna wants to say yes. Her mouth opens as if to say something, but it closes again, knowing that it would just get her in more trouble. If Ashanna makes her mother stop weeding and finds that she is lying, it will most certainly be a whooping. Accepting defeat, Ashanna releases the energy from her hand. What was up, comes down.

"Mh-hm, that is what I thought. Now, finish cleaning your room. As punishment for lying, you are going to help me weed the neighbor's garden."

"But Mother, I was supposed to do practice after I finished cleaning my room. Weeding old lady Millie's Garden will take all day, and I will not get to practice."

"I think you have had plenty of practice while you were supposed to be cleaning your room. Now, you better hurry because if I start weeding the neighbors' gardens before you can finish your room, there will be no practice tomorrow, either."

"That is not fair."

Myriusha gives a raised brow, silencing Ashanna. Myriusha pauses for a moment, seeing Ashanna's pleading eyes. In truth, she would rather have her practicing and learning than find some other way to get into trouble. "If you get everything done and weed the neighbor's garden before sundown..."

Ashanna interrupts with excitement, "You will let me practice twice as long tomorrow?"

"No, I was thinking we could write a letter together to Taritie. I am sure he will be amazed if you tell him all you are learning."

Ashanna's face begins to glow. "Really?"

"Here." Myriusha gestures for Ashanna to come close. Then, leaning her face toward Ashanna, they touch noses. "I promise." Retreating back out the window, she watches her little flower begin to hurry about the room, cleaning furiously. She finds herself like a mirthful child, remembering when she was little.

Taritie, returning to his station in the kingdom of Solis, finds himself being forced to take on apprentices. Despite Taritie's extended sojourn to the ruined capital, his fame for being a hero in the last war did not fade. Numerous pupils and young knights were thrust into his care over an eight-year period. His most recent apprentice, Ryonis, has been causing him immense headaches. During this time, he begins to receive letters from a certain young girl. This inspires him to go on "field research" with Ryonis.

All of the mighty trees of the land have turned from green to radiant gold. The side of the road has sparse red, blue, and purple trees. Running parallel to the road, two streams flow beside them with occasional waterfalls. The forest sometimes opens up with small glades, where previous travelers left firewood on the journey down.

In hindsight, Taritie wonders why he did not choose to return earlier. He misses spending his days in peace. The lives of Tyrnol and Myriusha are simple. In the capital of Solis, there is never peace. You meet your needs and then want more. Taritie imagines that the less you have, the simpler your life becomes, which is how he would like to live. That life could be in a house near theirs, where he can sit on the porch and rock himself to sleep.

A gust of wind blows along the road and pulls the leaves with its wake. The golden leaves descend over the two, and Taritie becomes entranced. To him, it is enough to ease the most restless soul... or so he wishes.

Ryonis, with a whiny groan, says, "Are we almost there? We have been traveling for nearly two weeks already."

Taritie, with no energy left, manages to stay awake through only willpower and leverages all his sanity and restraint. "We will arrive there shortly. We should be approaching the ruined city sometime today."

"Sometime today? Do you know what time today? Within a few hours, before midday, before nightfall?"

"I do not know, young lord." Taritie looks back and feels pain in his stomach. This boy reminds him of why he never wanted to marry or settle down. Despite how cute they look at a distance, children are a never-ending source of pain.

Ryonis, a young, white-haired, bratty child, rides on the back of his horse. He does not know the definition of the word "silence." Taritie has tried explaining to his father that the boy is far too emotional and soft to become a knight. Still, the father refuses to take him back. He has begged for the child to become a scholar, a priest, anything but a knight, but that is "beneath" a lord's son. If only they would understand the obnoxious complexities that lordship traps them in.

It is because of their pride that Taritie now journeys to the ruined city. With Ashanna's energy manipulator training, it may be possible to convince the Selestia-blooded brat to take on the path of an elemental technician. That way, Taritie would not have to deal with this high-maintenance child.

Taritie starts feeling rustling from behind him before Ryonis leaps from the horse. Taritie lets out a shout at him, but the boy keeps sprinting. Ahead of them, the town comes into view, and beyond that, the ruined capital. Taritie wants to ride to him, but he becomes distracted by pillars of smoke rising from the city. The ancient forges and machines of the ruined city have been reactivated.

His face turns from tired irritation to one of exhaustion. Why could the world not give him even a moment of a break? Just when he believed he could escape to this secluded place and rest, there is another new problem.

Taritie, seeing Ryonis approaching the turn they need to make, calls out, "The house we are going to is outside the village. It should have a large red Feylin tree in front of it." Thankfully, the boy pauses and leaves the road for a dirt path. Taritie spies the large foreign tree. For a moment, it seems the tree is swirling with red glowing bugs until he spies a little red-headed girl beneath the tree. Taritie sees her stop her artful practice and become tense. She quickly retreats behind her mother, who stands watch on the porch. Myriusha, eating a carrot from the garden, smiles at her daughter's sudden shyness. Taritie hears Myriusha call out a name. She then places the carrot on the patio of the house before walking out to meet the boy.

Taritie, unsurprised, hears the machine of his apprentice's mouth begin spitting before Myriusha can adequately introduce herself. His young, squeaky voice tries to talk a million words per second, and all of his attention is aimed at the young girl. "Good afternoon, my lady. I am Ryonis III of house Democritus."

Tyrnol comes out of the front door, waving toward Taritie. Taritie, having made it down the hill and to the house, greets them. "Morning, strangers."

Dismounting his horse, Tyrnol runs up to Taritie and gives him a hug. "It is a pleasure to see you again."

Warmth fills his cynical chest. "The pleasure is mine. How have you been?"

Myriusha, leaving Ashanna to the fate of being annoyed to death, comes over to join the conversation. "We are doing great. It has been too long since we last saw you, and we only received your letter that you were coming two days ago."

"Yes, I suppose I did leave in a hurry after sending it. To be honest, I needed a break from this little beast." Taritie gestures to the boy, who pesters Ashanna with unending questions. Ashanna, unable to take any more, runs back and resumes hiding behind her mom.

Myriusha laughs at the boy. "He has more energy than the town dogs. He is not yours by chance, is he?"

"No, thankfully." Taritie puts his arm around Ryonis and tucks him to his side.

Ryonis snaps back, "I am not that awful; Taritie is just a bad teacher. He does not want me to learn anything interesting."

"It is because you are too soft. You have amazing speed and talent, but you started crying because you damaged the straw dummy."

Tyrnol laughs and ruffles Ryonis' hair. "I am much the same. If softness is a weakness, you are not alone." Turning to Taritie, he asks, "Why bring him here with you, though?"

Taritie sighs and gestures toward Ashanna. "I figured the child could watch Ashanna practice. Selestia technicians are similar to Feylin manipulators, so I thought it may help the boy realize a new calling."

Myriusha pushes Ashanna forward excitedly. "That is a marvelous idea. Ashanna wanted to show you what she has learned." Ashanna digs her feet into the ground and grabs at her mother. All eyes turn to Ashanna.

Taritie, trying to make her feel better, saying, "I promise not to laugh at you. I came all this way to see what you have learned."

Ashanna closes her eyes, raising her hands. Energy flows through her body, gathering together in her hands and in her bare feet. From her feet, energy pours out like water, spreading over a flat surface. Her eyes open and glow with light. She points her hands toward the top of the hill, and a portal pops up. Energy flies out of her hands and creates a second portal near the tree in front of the house. Ashanna jumps through the portal by the tree and manifests near the road. Then, she jumps back through to reappear back at the tree.

Ashanna's parents start clapping and cheering. Taritie nods, which is how Taritie has been used to giving credit to someone's effort, but Myriusha takes it differently. "It may not be much now, but with practice, she will be able to do it quicker and will be able to teleport to places based on memory or sight."

Taritie, trying to assure her, giving her a warm smile. "I thought she did a wonderful job. Better than many I have seen her age." Myriusha examines Taritie's face to see if he is genuine but quickly gives up.

Ryonis displays much more emotion. Seeing her do it again, he lets out an audible "Woah!"

Taritie, realizing Myriusha's gaze lingering on him, starts clapping at Ashanna's second performance. Ashanna, seeing everyone smiling and clapping, swells with pride. She finally loses her shyness, confidently bragging, "Taritie, I am amazing, no?"

Ryonis goes up to Ashanna, and that shyness returns. She shrinks away from him. "I can tell you have put so much practice into this. You truly have a talent. It makes me curious, what else have you learned?"

Ashanna draws back at the question. Her eyes dart at Taritie, then Ryonis, then back at her parents. With more meekness than before, she starts to fiddle with her hands. "Well, I can move objects, create portals, and I can make my body float."

"That is awesome. Can you teach me how to do that stuff?"

Ashanna looks in surprise at him. She turns uncertainly to her mother, and Myriusha comes close to explain. "I am afraid not, Ryonis. You are a Selestia, you do not have the same energy pathways as the Feylin."

Taritie, seeing the desire and wonder in Ryonis, says, "Do not let her discourage you." Taritie grabs a jar and hands it over to Myriusha, who kneels beside Ryonis.

She rolls up the sleeve on his arm. She takes the gel from the jar, rubbing it on his forearm. After a moment, ice crystals begin sprouting from his skin. "While you may not be able to manipulate the world around you, it does not mean you are powerless. Selestia have powers we Feylin do not."

Ryonis looks up at Myriusha with wonder. "Like what?"

"Look at your hands. All I have done is touch the energy in your body, and it has reacted to me." Myriusha pulls back her hand, and fire begins spreading from his arm, melting the ice. Ryonis studies the water on his arm. Goosebumps appear, and he shivers before wiping off the water and patting the fire.

Ryonis feels his skin. "What was that?"

"Many Selestia have the power to control and manifest elements such as ice, fire, water, lightning, nature, air, and anything else you can imagine. We Feylin cannot do that."

"Do you think I could learn how to control elements?"

"Well, it is probably best to figure out what kind of technician you are. I think the test for figuring out your main element is included in a book I have inside. Do you want to go try it out?"

"I would love to." Myriusha rises, heading toward the house. Ashanna darts inside, Ryonis after her. However, when Taritie moves to head inside, Tyrnol grabs his arm. His eyes stare at the ground, and his hands are sweaty.

Taritie reflexively lowers his shoulder as if to swing off his sword but fights the reflex. Swallowing, he forces himself to calm down and listen. "How long are you staying?"

"I did not plan on staying long, but if you need something, I will do what I can." Taritie gestures toward the chairs on the porch. "Do you mind if we sit down and talk?"

"Not at all. You have been traveling for a while. How rude of me."

Sitting down on the front porch, Taritie waits for him, but he cannot help but see his eyes drifting toward the smoke rising in the distance.

Myriusha pops her head out, placing down a plate of cookies before heading back inside. Tyrnol jokingly grabs the plate and begins to stuff his face before offering them to Taritie. Both of them get a laugh, but Taritie still feels uneasy. A gnawing feeling grows more intense in the back of his mind.

Tyrnol finishes chewing. Clearing his throat, he says, "How is preventing the war going?"

Taritie grabs a cookie and takes a small bite. Looking out across the peaceful town, it is hard for Taritie to imagine the terrors that are happening, likely at this very moment. Though, the last person he believed would be affected by the conflict would be Tyrnol. "War has been declared by the kingdom of Nocturna on Solis. Sooner or later, I will be called to fight. I only hope that Ryonis will not have to."

"If this is what the boy has chosen, you should encourage him not to fight against it."

"I still remember my first time taking a life. I would never wish that feeling upon anyone. It will ruin that boy's soft heart. He will become a completely different creature entirely."

"I cannot say I have ever killed anyone, so I cannot offer good advice. I can only say if it is inevitable, all you can do is prepare him for it."

"The first man I killed, I did it in revenge. I am still able to recall the surprise, terror, and pride I felt. The most dominant feeling was the short burst of pride." Taritie finishes his cookie and leans back in his chair. "Next, I remember his eyes glassing over and staring back at me. The way his hollowed eyes somehow reflected my own. The cold shiver of my blood turning cold, and the sickening sensation rising directly from my gut." Taritie realizes he is letting himself get carried away. He has never admitted any of this aloud before. Some of this he confronts for the first time himself.

Taritie wants to examine the scene more but chooses to let it go. Letting out a sigh and looking up to watch the birds, his mind thinks of how the birds do not wage war. In the sky, they are free from the horrible fate that sapient creatures can never escape from.

"With how young you are, I am almost scared to wonder what age you first took a life. In some ways, it makes me understand more of the strange way you carry yourself."

"I carry myself strange?"

"I mean that you act older than you are. You do not give me the impression of a young hero."

Taritie says, "I know Ryonis will face bloodshed whether I train him or not. However, it does not give me any solace." He pauses, grabbing another cookie. "If the war in Solis goes bad and it arrives on your front porch, they could ask your daughter to serve because she is a capable manipulator. Would you not fight against it?"

"Yes, I would fight that. I would even offer myself to go in her place."

"And if they chose to take you both?"

"You are sounding like a father yourself, Taritie."

"No, I am no father, but this child is innocent. To properly train him, I would have to take that innocence away. How can I live with myself having done that?"

"You have to because it is your responsibility."

There is a gap of silence between the two. Taritie wants to continue to argue, but his heart is no longer in it. He is weary, and more pressing questions are weighing on him. His eyes drift back to the smoke coming from the chimneys in the ruined capital.

Taritie points to the ruined city. "How long?"

"You mean the smoke? It started about a month after the machinery first started up. That was about last fall or winter." Tyrnol's eyes squint and become serious. "There are rumors the capital is reactivating, and within a few years, the gate will open again."

"Reactivating?"

"Yeah, a Feylin research team came out here a week ago. They hovered as high as they could, all of them trying to see inside. They say that the time-frozen chambers are unlocking, new creatures are being released, machine creations are walking to and fro, and the most outlandish of the rumors is that while they were floating, they saw an ancient Shappalan."

"An ancient Shappalan? That would mean he comes

directly from the end of the great war."

"Yeah, you are Shappalan, too, are you not?"

"Well, yeah, but my bloodline is not from the Great War or anything. My ancestors were frozen during the time before the war by the nation of Selestia. The same time as yours and everyone else's ancestors. Not to mention, everyone had their immortality revoked before being frozen."

"Why are you so defensive? All I asked was if you had the same blood. However, after you came and helped us, I asked my family up north if they had ever seen any Shappalans before. Do you want to know the interesting thing they told me?"

Before Tyrnol could finish, Myriusha opened the house door, startling Taritie and announcing, "Your son, Ryonis, is an ice technician. You should come and see for yourself. He was able to manifest frost on his palm all on his own."

Myriusha realizes that something is up, and Tyrnol assures Taritie. "Do not worry. I will not bring it up again. Everyone has their secrets for a reason."

Myriusha's eyes perk up. She stares back and forth at Taritie and Tyrnol curiously. "What secret? Is Ryonis really his son?"

Taritie protests, "No, that is not the case at all." Taritie's face turns beet red. Feeling uncomfortable with Ryonis on one side and Myriusha on the other, he rises. "How about I check in on Ryonis?"

Myriusha leaves the door open and gestures for her husband to come inside, but he raises his hand and replies, "I want to stay out here a moment longer." Loud talking and celebrating can be heard inside. Tyrnol does not hear it over his own thoughts. Like a beating drum, his mind races more audible than any noise they could make. He stares off into the smoke pillars and wonders what the future will hold.

CHAPTER THREE: TECHNICIAN

In the spring of the seventh year of the Feylin Calendar, Taritie and Ryonis return home to the city of Solbrond. Arriving home they discover lords and banners, marching away to distant frontlines. In their month-long leave, the Nocturna Empire penetrated the northern and western boundaries.

The kingdom of Solis obtained a few victories early on, but time leans in Nocturna's favor. With a lucky break, they surround the city of Solbrond, tear down its walls, and capture their king.

"Ryonis, help me barricade the door." Taritie grasps a bench and throws it against the door. Ryonis lifts a hand and grabs onto a table. With help from two other soldiers, he helps drag the heavy wooden table to block the door.

A soldier with a wounded arm asks Taritie, "Do you think that will hold?"

Taritie wipes the sweat off his brow. His eyes feel heavy

enough to drag the rest of him tumbling to the floor. His arms burn, and his legs feel ready to give out from under him. His plans fell short at the wall. The men he led, their bodies scattered in the courtyard. The king he defended, captured, and dragged away. He is not even lucky enough to die with honor and pride.

Taritie glances over at the man who addressed him. He has seen this man before. A cocky boy, who dreamt of glory. Now, his face looks horrified, and his eyes glaze over as he shakes. What does he expect of Taritie, to give him hope where there is none?

Taritie fights against his pessimism, saying, "There is hope. Somewhere in this study is a passage outside. The door only needs to last until we find it."

The soldiers finish barricading the door. Taking off their helmets, they comb the small room for any semblance of a secret passage. While searching, Ryonis, looking pale, starts conservation with a hallowed voice. "Hard to imagine that in my lifetime, I would see the end of the kingdom of Solis."

Taritie feels along the wall. He pounds the stone and listens. "None could have imagined the numbers by which their drakes descended. Our walls made obsolete before them." He glances over to Ryonis. He takes a seat on a lone chair, trembling, covering his head. The sound of sobbing can be heard from him.

Taritie, feeling the last of the wall, turns to Ryonis. He

may bear the markings of a soldier, but he is still just a child. Taritie rests his hand on Ryonis' shoulder. Ryonis begins to weep, desperately covering his eyes so as not to let Taritie see.

With his face turned away and covered, through sobbing, he moans, "I can still see the view in my mind. Drakes descending from the sky, burning my family's home with no warning. My mother, father, sister, and now me. Is there no mercy in this world?"

Taritie remembers words similar to Ryonis'. Taritie wraps his arm around the boy and holds him, saying, "I imagine that it seems that the body has lost all warmth to you."

Releasing him, Taritie stands up to face the knights that surround them. Having combed the room, they look to Taritie for hope. Ryonis, wiping his tears and removing his technician's hat, stands up facing them.

"Why are you all looking to Taritie to save us? Are we not all men of Solis?" The soldiers look to Ryonis and then each other. "Until the memory of our nation dies from our hearts, this land is not taken. Grasp what courage you have, and if there is no escape, face your death with pride."

Taritie watches, speechless, as Ryonis discovers something from inside of him. The worry from his face is not gone and neither is the fear, however, he has awakened somehow. The child did not desire to even take a life, yet now he takes command of soldiers, commanding these broken few to once more reignite their hope.

Taritie takes another look at Ryonis. Part of him still resembles that young boy. He wears a soft fur-like mane around his neck. Robes of grey and white, coated in filth, adorn him. Around his waist are strips of cloth similar to banners, each with unique symbols that bless him with boons.

Taritie finds a renewed burst of strength in himself. How can he let his apprentice take charge while he sulks? He rises and checks the hallway beyond the barricade. He looks through a small stained-glass window. Shadows move and draw close. Taritie whispers to himself, "I swear to you, Ryonis, I will get you out of this place. You will not burn here. For the lives of your family, you will continue their bloodline."

A soldier sits down on the seat, saying, "No more. It is hopeless. Just let them come and kill us now."

Ryonis turns from his search. "Not yet. If we have to, we will rip down this wall and make a path."

The soldier hangs his head. "I just want to give up. If you tell me to die, I will gladly fall on my blade and find peace. Instead, your words are stones on my already crushed body."

Taritie approaches the man and rests his hand on him. "It is for that reason you must continue. For your family, for your brothers that lie dead, for the fact there is still breath in our lungs."

Shouts rise from beyond the barricade. The room goes silent. Footsteps echo from the halls, and nearby doors are forced open. A cacophony of screams fills the ears of the men. The barricaded door rattles softly and crescendos into banging and yelling.

Three men rush to the door, using their weight to brace against the invaders. Ryonis glances toward Taritie, who unslings his sword. Taritie gives a nod to Ryonis. Resolved, Ryonis pulls from his satchel a leather book with an iron clasp.

Taritie stands tall and takes charge of the situation. "Those with swords stand to the side, spears front and center, bows in the far rear." With Ryonis at his side, Taritie orders, "Ryonis, at your discretion, send forth the strongest icy wind you can muster."

The wood of the door begins to splinter and crack as an enemy axe peaks through. Hands appear, ripping out loose boards. Taritie grabs a spear, shoving it through a crack in the door. He pulls back the spear, now tipped with blood, handing it off to a soldier near him.

The leader of the archers, Nathan, says to Taritie, "Sir, would you help me for a moment?"

"What is it?" Taritie turns to see Nathan pointing down to the rug on the floor. Taritie nods his head, moving to one side of the rug. They throw the carpet to the side, revealing cold scratched stone.

Nathan's shoulders slowly sag. "I am sorry, that was the last place I could think of."

"I find myself learning lessons in hope; now let this old dog teach you a lesson in patience."

Taritie cocks his eye at Nathan before grinning and dropping to the ground. He feels the scratches that lead toward the fireplace, where fresh soot is littered on the floor. Someone had recently displaced the cinder-rocks inside the heath.

Taritie calls out, "Ryonis, come and give me some cold air."

Ryonis looks to Taritie with bewilderment. "The enemy is about to break in."

"All the more reason you should hurry over here."

"I do not see how putting out the hearth will help us."

"Ryonis!"

Ryonis opens his book, flips to the marked page, and blows cold air onto the fire. Taritie reaches his gauntleted hand into the hearth. He pulls out the grate and shovels rock onto the floor. He sees an unusually large stone in the back of the hearth. Gripping the large stone with abnormal strength, he pulls it from the fireplace, revealing a tunnel to the outside. Taritie grabs Ryonis, shakes him, and kisses his forehead.

Taritie announces, "Everyone, get into the hearth and get out of here. I will be holding off the enemy."

The soldiers, without hesitation, begin rushing to the hearth. Knights in full armor flop on the ground to wiggle through the grand hearth. The only one to stand still is Ryonis, who faces Taritie. "Alone? You cannot hold them back by yourself."

"I have come to a decision; we are all living." Taritie gives a reassuring smile while the enemy continues tearing apart the door, trying to get through.

"I will not abandon you." Ryonis continues to stand beside him. With his book still open, frost gathers on his free hand.

"No. Go through the hearth with the others. I will not risk losing you."

"Neither will I risk you."

Taritie looks flustered. "That is not the point. I have chosen to defend you all."

"I have chosen to be with you. Are we not both knights of Solis? Did we not take oaths to defend our kingdom?"

"I am trying to protect you. Why are you such a fool?"

"Why are you so stubborn? If my kingdom is gone, all that is left of my oath is to defend my brothers. I will not flee from this." The door is torn from its hinges and thrown to the ground. A group of soldiers rush into the room, pushing the table and other furniture out of the way. Behind them, twenty more soldiers wait expectantly.

"Fine, I concede, fight with me, Ryonis. Push these fiends back to the main hall. Let us show these night lovers that there is still warmth in the sun."

Ryonis meditates on the words of his book, unleashing a great gale of cold wind. The blast of wind blows through the hallway until ice builds on the enemy helmets and feet. Their noses turn blue, and even their eyes begin to develop crystals. The cold wind encases the soldiers to the point their movements become rigid and slow. The enemies moan aloud with desperate pleas. The laughing mob devolves into a shivering mess.

Taritie rushes against them. Throwing what little remains of the barricade out of the way, he unleashes his great sword on the enemy. He slices through four enemies and grasps their bodies to throw them out of his path. Two soldiers try to strike at him, but they do not have the movement to hit the swift knight. With a mighty swing, their bodies erupt in blood.

The soldiers in the hallway begin to move faster as their freedom of movement returns. Taritie lowers his blade and rushes into the hallway. As he runs, an ice spike flies past his shoulders and pierces the skull of an enemy. Another spike whizzes by and misses, but the next hits its mark.

Taritie realizes that there may be hope left in this kingdom. For even as each enemy rushes at him, it only adds another body to line the floor until all have been felled. He looks for more enemies, but none seem to be there. Only a roar that draws out his curiosity.

With Ryonis behind him, Taritie peaks open the door to the great hall. Looking into the hall, he sees countless enemy soldiers filling the room. They listen to a speech from their commander. The men in the room are distracted with a morbid glee plastered on their faces. He hears an audible gasp from Ryonis, and he looks for the source of his surprise. That is when he notices that the head of their king is in the grip of the enemy commander's hand.

Taritie closes the door and places his hand on Ryonis' shoulder. "Come, there is nothing more for us here."

They return, entering the passage inside the hearth. The dark and rank-smelling tunnel did not look like the smell of freedom, but it was at least hope for another day. Then, they reach the end of the passage. Splayed before the exit are the bodies of their brothers, slaughtered at its entrance.

Ryonis stares horrified. "Riley, Thomas, Mar..."

Taritie flashes out his hand to Ryonis. "Quiet now."

Slowly moving forward, Taritie peers beyond the exit. In the light, he sees a group of soldiers laugh as they play games with a captured knight. One soldier approaches the knight and removes his helmet, revealing Nathan. They take turns throwing knives at him. Taritie watches helplessly, doing nothing as one enters his neck. His head lowers, lifeless. From the soldiers, he hears, "Oh, you broke our toy! Now who will we have fun with?"

In anger, Ryonis pushes away from Taritie. He whips open his technician's book. He sends forth a cold wind that slows the group. Ryonis kicks down a knight near him and begins pummeling him. Taritie rushes out of the passage after him. Taritie guards Ryonis' back against the soldiers. Ryonis attaches his book to his waist and pulls out a pair of daggers. He stabs the soldier under him and charges at the twelve frozen soldiers. He rampages through the group. He murders each one of them and shouts to the sky. He slumps forward in a daze.

Taritie guides Ryonis' hands down. He sets Ryonis against a stump and pries away his daggers, sheathing them. Ryonis pulls out his book and begins to hug it with white knuckles. His eyes shift back to his fallen friends, and he turns halfhearted to Taritie. "Why do they take everything away from us? This passage was meant to be hopeful, and they murdered everyone who came through. It took us forever to find it, and they were just waiting out here. If we had gone with our friends, we would be dead just like them."

Taritie wants to reassure him, but he can think of nothing. He reaches for Ryonis, grabbing his head, and holding him close. Taritie shifts his hand through the young boy's dirty hair. They stay that way for a time until a cry from someone interrupts them. Ryonis moves his hands toward one of his daggers, but Taritie stops him.

He separates himself from Ryonis. Patting his back, Taritie moves to the source. Reluctantly, Ryonis follows. Hiding inside a bush, their eyes spy a lone woman before roughly fifty enemy knights. Ryonis spies the colors of white and royal blue on her gown. Few could ever afford such colors, and they happen to be the colors of the royal family of Solis. The soldiers surround her, poking her and mocking her like predators playing with food.

Ryonis feels a pulse of anger like a throbbing pain in his head. His hatred is transparent. Despite his exhaustion, his eyes turn toward Taritie. "We have to do something about this."

"We cannot take on that many enemies. Even if you did freeze them, we are both tired and in no shape to fight. Look at yourself; your eyes hang low, and your silver hair fades to black."

"That is no excuse. That is the princess."

"I couldn't care less who she is. This kingdom is dying, and I will not risk your life for anyone else's."

"Wait, I just may have a plan."

Ryonis flips through his book. While he does, a group of guards seem to have noticed the commotion. They near their position. Before Taritie can leap out of the bushes, Ryonis raises his hand. A great chill wind leaves the bushes and begins to form something with ice. The enemy ignores the girl, with their commander grabbing a hold of her. The commander shouts, "Kill him before the technician can finish!"

Taritie leaps from the bush and parries the first enemy. The man falls to his feet. The second knight's blade hits Taritie, bouncing from his plate and sliding off. Taritie drops his greatsword, grabs the arm of the enemy knight, draws a dagger off his waist, and thrusts it into the knight. Taritie pushes away the knight and sees the entire horde upon him.

The knights close in, but before they can reach him, a gust of wind comes swirling between him and the enemy. From that wind, an ice golem stands tall in the shape of an owl bear. The golem charges to attack the enemy, pushing them back. The attention of all the knights gravitates to the golem, giving Ryonis the chance to circle around them. He begins moving toward the back and eyes the princess. Taritie attempts to follow Ryonis but is cut off by enemies. He becomes back-to-back with the golem fighting the horde.

Ryonis stabs the back of the enemy commander. He grabs the princess and runs. Ryonis does not stay to finish the commander but escapes into the woods. Taritie, noticing Ryonis fleeing, cuts through an enemy and uses his body to shove his way out of the horde. He throws the body to the side and sprints away.

Many of the knights stay focused on the golem, but the enemy commander alerts them, saying, "Do not let them escape. Fetch the horses."

Taritie attempts to catch up with Ryonis. Unfortunately, his heavy armor slows him down, making it impossible. Ryonis takes notice and slows his pace. With barely any breath, Taritie says, "Well, you were worried about where we would go. Now, you do not have to worry. They have seen our faces, and now, I tell you, they will surely hunt us down wherever we are."

Ryonis, with a smile on his face, proposes, "What if they are not able to get to us? Even if they know where we are."

"What are you talking about?"

"The ruined capital."

CHAPTER FOUR: SCHOLAR

A light rain falls down from the new moon sky. Having spent a day evading and traversing the hilly landscape of Solis, and with a week still ahead, Taritie chooses to rest. Underneath the overhead of a large stone, he stokes a large fire despite the damp conditions.

Ryonis took quickly to sleep but violently squirms with mutterings escaping his lips. A horrid sweat covers his body and drenches his clothes. Taritie longs to help the boy, but he can do nothing as the boy faces this trial alone. He gently runs his hand along Ryonis' back. With each of his nightmares, Taritie begins a new prayer. As the cycle continues, it becomes apparent to Taritie that a change is happening in himself as well. The days of his own youth come to his mind. When he was all alone. How much he would have given to have someone come and pick him back up. He could be to this boy the Father that he no longer has... He pushes away the strange thought. The boy is his apprentice, and with how much effort Taritie has put into this boy, it is only natural that he cares for him. It is not his place to be anything more, and neither does he want that responsibility.

Taritie's hand moves his hand up and begins massaging Ryonis' scalp. To Taritie's relief, this seems to bring him comfort. Taritie runs his hands through his greasy hair. He pauses for a moment, bunching together the strands. The silver of his hair had yet to return. Despite days passing, his hair is darker than the charred coals that burn in the fire. Somehow, he does not imagine it will return until the terrors over him pass.

The "princess" Salie, whom Ryonis had saved, sits down after scavenging in the woods. From her empty hands, it seems it did not go as she wanted. She, whom Ryonis believed to be the king's daughter, in reality, was born lower than he assumed. Despite her stunning looks and knowledge of the secret passage, she is only an assistant to the royal court's scholar. She fled with the scholars through the secret passage. They were ambushed, and she attempted to return to the city.

Salie shifts just a moment, causing Taritie to look up to her. She looks like she wants to ask a question but shyness claims her voice. In nervousness she reaches down and plays with the fringes of her clothes. Her clothes, dyed in royal blue and white, are like robes that identify as a dress. Around her neck is an expensive scarf with cuts and what look to be teeth marks from some creature.

Finding her voice, she asks, "So, Taritie is your name, right?"

Taritie is encouraged to find she has more strength in her voice than days previously. "Yes, that is my name, and this is Ryonis."

"He already introduced himself to me. It was you who seemed to avoid introductions." She plays with her beautiful silver hair. Her hair is similar to Ryonis', but she has striking bright orange eyes that distinguish her from his icy blue ones.

"Yes, sorry about that." Taritie releases Ryonis' head. He positions himself closer to the fire.

"To be blunt, I do not care. What I care about is that boy's groaning. I am impressed the enemy is not already on top of us with how loud he is."

Taritie stops looking her up and down, and it registers that she just insulted Ryonis. "I know you are angry but do not take it out on the boy. What each of us experienced during the siege is horrible, and we will all have our scars from it."

"The enemy would not need good trackers if every night that boy is going to be wailing."

"What about you?"

"What do you mean? You do not hear me crying."

"I am impressed then. I figured that you were a fragile

scholar's apprentice. I mean, you watched all your friends and teachers die. Then, you were played with like a toy by those knights."

Salie fidgets her hands, no longer seeming comfortable to leave them resting. "What are you getting at?"

"Nothing, but imagine what would have happened if we did not come to your rescue."

Salie's eyes drift away. She grips her shaking arm and mutters something under her breath. She shakes herself and then looks away from Taritie with disinterest.

Taritie finds himself feeling ashamed. He did not want to hurt her, but she set him off, as he had already been on edge for another reason. He has never been confident in conversations with women, especially women he finds attractive.

She is a young beauty, likely in her twenties. Her orange eyes have captivated him from the moment he saw them. The unnatural color and design remind him of his own people's golden eyes. What he would give to see a woman with golden eyes staring at him.

While looking at her, Taritie notices she is fiddling with something in her hand. Something that looks like dried pellets of some kind. "What is it you are holding?"

"Why do you care?" She wraps her fingers around the pellet, obscuring it.

"I am sorry for being rude. I think we both said things we did not intend."

She arrogantly rolls her eyes. "Anyways, you were curious about this?" She puts the pellet near the fire. "It is a dragon pellet. My grandmother taught me how to make them."

Taritie takes note of the symbol on her shoulder and around her neck. The symbol of the scholarly community. "Food for a pet dragon?" Taritie looks with intrigue and moves closer to the fire. He reaches out, and she gives him a pellet. He looks it over, studying the dried food. "What kind of dragon is it?"

"She is a miniature red wyvern. I adore her." She respectfully takes the pellet back.

"What happened to it? Did it die in the battle yesterday?"

"No, I do not think so. I told her to fly off and watch me from a distance. I have occasionally seen her, but she has yet to return to me."

"Will she starve if you are not feeding her?"

"No, she is able to hunt well enough on her own. There is plenty of game in these parts. She does not return because our hunters are still near."

"I see." Taritie yawns and Salie responds with an even larger yawn. "Go ahead and get some sleep. It is still a week and a half-journey to the ruined capital. Perhaps longer, since we are trying to throw off our pursuers."

Rynois, each time he awakes, changes little by little. The way he carries himself is more somber. His eyes were darker, his movements heavy, and at night, even during his most restless nights, he refused to scream. Taritie expects him to revert to his normal self, but throughout the journey, he only grows colder. Taritie doubts that there is anything that could bring out the passion and energy in him anymore, except...

A small familiar house on the outskirts of town, covered in a light dusting of snow. The leaves of the great red tree are gone, and the branches have little piles of snow. The moment Taritie and Ryonis step on the path, a familiar but much taller girl bursts out from the house. With her new height, she has managed to outgrow Ryonis. Red horns sprout from her head, surrounded by long, combed, curly hair. Throughout her body, her energy paths glow with a dark red and complement her tan skin.

Ashanna grins at Ryonis and Taritie. "It is so good to see you! How have you been?"

Ryonis replies with a cool and calm tone, "Not the best, but I will survive."

Ashanna looks worried and gets up in his face, studying him closely and causing him to blush. "What is wrong? You can tell me anything."

Taritie ruffles his salt-and-peppered apprentice's hair, saying, "I think it is best if we discuss it inside with your parents present." Taritie notices a darkening on her face. He knows that look well. Ryonis has had the same expression on his own face for days.

Ashanna gives a forced smile and says, "Of course, come right on in."

Taritie gestures for Salie to follow, and all of them go inside. Ashanna seats everyone and holds out a basket of raisins. After each grabs a few, she places it before them. Ashanna calls out to her Father, "Taritie and Ryonis have come to visit. Do you need some help?"

"No, I am on my way."

They see a door open, and Tyrnol steps out. Taritie has to take a moment to make sure he sees the same man as before. His left leg is gone, his right eye is blind with a large scar, and multiple deformities cover his body that can be seen through the old and worn clothes.

Taritie jumps from his seat and tries to help Tyrnol to a seat. Tyrnol gestures for him to sit down and continues to walk using a wooden cane. "What happened to you, my friend?"

After sitting down, Tyrnol answers, "Well, I got into something that was a little over my head."

Taritie sits back down, leaning in close. "What took place that could have done this to you, and where is Myriusha?"

"You do not know? Have the happenings here not reached the capital? What of my letters?"

"If you want your letters, I would ask the Nocturna empire. The capital has been hard-pressed to receive intel reports, let alone letters, these last months."

"Let me catch you up on the current times, then. The gate to the ruined capital has opened. People from distant lands came flooding into the capital, and soon, a large expedition was being formed. Scholars attached to Myriusha's family came and begged us to join them." Tyrnol gripped his cane until his knuckles turned white. "At first, everything seemed docile and nice. The machines helped us inside, and the creatures were small and harmless. That was all the case until we came too far to turn back. That was when they ambushed us. Monsters of great size and hordes of smaller creatures hunted us as if it were a game. We tried to escape underground, but nowhere was safe. Underneath the earth, machines, and beasts, as if mentally linked, tracked us down. It was chaos and in that chaos... Myriusha was taken from me."

"Tyrnol..." Taritie looks toward Ashanna. Her eyes

appear glassy and distant.

"For weeks, we were stuck down there until we found a way out. By then, the large expedition, near a thousand of us, had become less than a dozen. I barely made it out with my life."

Ashanna's eyes become watery, and she closes them. "Enough of us, what brings you here?"

Taritie looks over to Ryonis. He fears that Ashanna needs to hear something uplifting, but he has no such news. "Solis has fallen, and the nation of Nocturna will soon be coming through these lands to claim them."

Tyrnol slams his fist on the table, "We came to this land to escape those bastards. Those barbarians slaughter and rule over others without any compassion. I was worried how I would survive the winter the way I am, let alone if they came to raid my home."

Taritie's heart reaches out for his friend. He feels his pain as if it is his own. "I am sorry, I wish I had better news."

"No, I knew the moment Ashanna told me you had arrived it meant ill tides. The only question is, what are your plans now that you are here?"

Taritie opens his mouth to say something, but he hesitates after hearing Tyrnol's story. To Taritie's surprise, Ryonis speaks up. "We will head into the Ruined capital, and we will find a way to survive there."

"I should have guessed." Tyrnol looks with burdened eyes on Ryonis. Eventually, his gaze meets Taritie's. The look conveys to Taritie a question that he puts into words for Ryonis. "Is that the only path you can see? Do you believe the ruined capital is your only hope?"

Taritie answers his friend, saying, "You know it as well as I do. The south is nothing but ocean, and the east is the Green Feylin kingdom. If we tried to step foot in that territory, they would kill us both for trespassing. That leaves only the kingdom of Nordis to the northeast, but they despise the Selestians and would not allow Ryonis in their land. However, even if we were to journey to these lands, we would never reach them. We are being hunted, and we can run for only so long."

Tyrnol points his cane up toward the pantry. "Ashanna, pack as much food as we have left, and give it to them."

Ashanna looks pleadingly toward her Father. She drops down at his knees. "Father, without that food, we cannot survive the winter."

"Survive? What is in that pantry will not keep us. That is why you will go with Taritie and Ryonis."

"What? You expect me to leave you, Father?"

Taritie seems nearly as shocked by the suggestion as Ashanna. "My friend, I cannot guarantee her safety."

"This is not up for discussion. I will go and join the

church. There, I will help with what little I can do. There, I may survive longer than I would otherwise. With luck, I may survive to see spring and the coming of Nocturna's rule. However, if you join me… the daughter of a beggar is no life. Not any life I want for you."

"Father, do you seriously believe I would sacrifice you for anything? I would rather be by your side. You know that."

Tyrnol turns back to Taritie and sternly says, "You will watch after my daughter. You will not let her leave your sight. As long as you are there, I know she will be okay."

Taritie does not know how to respond. One would imagine that the world itself was unraveling. "I already have Ryonis under my care. I am unable to promise even his safety."

"You will give me your word, Taritie, or I will curse you with all of what remains of my soul."

Taritie wordlessly stares at his pitiful friend. In resignation, he agrees. "You have my word. I will do all in my power to keep her safe. May the creator witness me that as I breathe, any who threaten their life will die by my hand."

Salie for the first time pipes in, asking, "Why are you so confident that Taritie will survive where a thousand failed?"

"Because he has been there before." Tyrnol does not elaborate, his eyes glued to Taritie. The others' eyes follow his penetrating gaze, and there is a choking silence.

Opening up the veil of quiet, Ryonis says, "You told me you could not find a way inside. Why did you lie? What did you find in there?"

Taritie runs his hand through his hair. His mind races for some way to get out of this situation.

Ryonis keeps pressing Taritie for answers while Salie gains courage. The moment she can get her voice in, she overpowers Ryonis in terms of volume, asking, "What was it like inside? Was it as dangerous as Tyrnol says it is? How did you survive...?"

Ashanna stands up from her chair with tears in her eyes and quietly rushes out of the house. Ryonis looks toward Taritie, his eyes saying that he is divided between staying and going after her. He finally decides to get up and runs after her. Before he can leave, Taritie grabs his arm. "Give her some space. I think she wants to be alone right now."

Ryonis brushes off his arm. "Unlike someone, I am not going to just leave her alone with her thoughts. I think I understand more than anyone needing someone who will just listen."

Tyrnol clears his throat to gain their attention. "She has had months to be alone. Let the boy go after her." Taritie steps away from Ryonis. Tyrnol gives a nod to the boy, saying, "Just be careful what you say, and make sure to listen more than talk."

With the two children gone, Salie takes the chance to press her questions. "What was it like inside the ruined capital? You have to tell me. it is a mystery as old as Solis."

Taritie gently asks, "Do you mind if I have a moment with my friend here?"

"That is so mundane." She rolls her eyes before making for the door. "I guess I can find something to do."

With everyone gone, there is a pleasant peace in the room. Taritie eats a few raisins and seems to be fine, enjoying the quiet. Looking out the window, he can see Salie pulling out a book and practicing some sort of language, which must be some ancient or otherwise old script.

Tyrnol scratches his scruffy beard. "I am sorry for mentioning you have been to the capital before. I knew the moment it left my mouth, I was going to regret it."

Taritie finishes chewing a mouthful of raisins, swallows, and sighs. "You are right though, I did not want anyone to know but yes, I have been inside the ruined capital before. How many millennia has taken place since then, I have no clue."

"It is true then, you are an immortal. The last immortal."

"I do not know if I am the last. I know I have walked this earth and not found another. However, that does not mean there could not be another. More than likely, there is one that remains inside the ruined capital."

"Outstanding, to have lived during an age of harmony and peace. Where Death's fangs had been filed to the point of nearly disappearing forever."

"When a sheep looks across a divide and sees other sheep, I wonder what it imagines the life on the other side is like."

"What are you trying to say?"

"Death's fangs were never filed down. No, its diet just became selective." A dark look comes across Taritie's face. His demeanor changes, and for a second, Tyrnol looks upon the face of a different man. Taritie says, "I see in your face the envy you have for me, but I tell you it is wrongly placed."

"How can you say that? I have read and studied the ancient inscriptions myself. They detail that everyone who is born is given immortality." Tyrnol's face looks longingly, and it hurts Taritie to the point he cannot stand. Tyrnol longs to have his wife back, but he has no clue what he is desiring. He does not understand the price that is paid, and his confusion is only building the longer Taritie says nothing. "Taritie, do not treat me like a child; what is it you are not telling me?"

"When I first met you, you two reminded me of my parents living in the gutters of a colony moon in the middle of nowhere. No money to their name, moving to an unfamiliar place and hoping for the best. They did not care about the cost when they chose to give birth to a child. However, in the golden age that you long for, they committed the cardinal sin. It was not long before they were taken, and my sister and I were left on the streets of that colony with nothing." Taritie notices a familiar necklace on a small table against the far wall. He gets up and walks over to his mother's necklace, recalling the day he gave it to Ashanna.

"They took your parents away? You were never able to see each other again. Forgive me for bringing up these bad memories."

"Stop it, my friend. You have no need to apologize to me." Taritie brings the necklace over to the table and sits back down. He feels the shape of the crown of diamonds on the pendant and feels its familiar shape and it calms him down.

"Did you ever try to see your parents again?" Taritie looks up at him, and he understands, in his mind, that he is trying to relate.

"That was not possible."

"Why not?"

"It just was not possible." Taritie brings his hands to his face. His mind is screaming. Why is his friend so persistent in knowing this?

Once more, Tyrnol presses, saying, "Are you saying you were immortal, and you never tried?"

The last bits of Taritie snap. "Do you seriously believe

that I had that ability? They did not take my parents away; they murdered them!" What looks to be sprouts of green cinders appear from the air around Taritie. They gather along Taritie's blade as if he is preparing to strike down someone. They are different from any flame Tyrnol has seen before, and they give off an air that they would burn more than just flesh.

Taritie remembers a scene that he has tried to forget for so long. The day he froze himself away. The blood that poured off his hands. Green flames that burned all around him. "In return, I..." Taritie goes wordless for a moment. He slams his hands down on the table and lowers his head.

Tyrnol rises from his seat. With effort, he hobbles over to Taritie. He pulls out the chair that Ryonis was sitting in, and he takes a seat down. Reaching out his hand, he places it on Taritie's. "I want you to forgive me, my friend. I made assumptions about you that were not fair."

"No, I need you to forgive me." Taritie avoids Tyrnol's gaze. How could he let those memories resurface again? Why will they not stay buried? How is it that no length of time will let him forget? He only wants to be free, and yet the flame is still with him. What if Tyrnol asks about that flame? No, his friend can never know. No one can ever know about that secret. He needs to gain a better grip on his emotions. The memories need to be locked away. He had believed those memories to already have been locked away. The seal he has kept on them is coming loose.

"That anger in your eyes, I feel it inside of me. Aching loss that burns like fire."

"I thought time would cool the flame."

"My friend, I do not believe some flames can be doused so easily. After all, I never want to forget my love for her. However, if I continue to love her, I will continue to miss her."

"Then what can you do to be free of the hurt?"

"I do not know myself. You would think, with how long you lived, I could ask you for the answer."

Taritie finds himself laughing despite himself. "I wish that was true. It seems the opposite is true. The longer I live, the less I feel I know."

"As a parent, Ashanna will ask me so many questions, and I will not know the answer to many of them. Though, I find when I talk it through with her, I learn as she learns."

"I have never talked about this to anyone."

"I was not meaning to guilt you into talking. Friend, if you are not comfortable talking, wait until you are."

Taritie awkwardly nods his head. He grabs a few more raisins. While he eats, he notices Tyrnol fidgeting quite a bit. He imagines that his past was not the only thing that he was curious about.

Tyrnol swallows and musters his courage, asking, "What did we do wrong inside the capital? Why did everything turn against us?"

"Truthfully, I do not have a clue. I was sealed before the war that ended all life. In my lifetime, most were still immortal. In fact, those frozen in time should have remained immortal." Taritie takes a breath, and he has so many questions about what happened. Questions he fears will be answered inside the capital. "Back then, the capital was just a regular city. After I was sealed, the war broke out, and Shappala found an easy-to-produce cure against immortality. How they did it and how they distributed it, I do not know. I only knew that when I awoke in this world, everything had changed. At some point, they must have injected the cure into those frozen away, which is why I remain immortal. I was not with them."

"Do you think there is a way to reverse what has happened to the city, to make it peaceful again?"

"That, I do know. Whatever has become of the city is the result of someone inside. The city is similar to a sentient creature, and it is influenced by the control towers, command room, and the heart of the city. If the city has become a dangerous place, it is because the person controlling the city, likely in the command room, is likewise dangerous."

"That means it is almost certain someone is still alive in

there."

"For the city to awaken as it has… yes, someone is most certainly alive."

"You fear discovering the past. Will you still enter the capital despite your fears?"

"I do not have a choice. Ryonis, Salie, and now Ashanna are in my care. If it comes to protecting them and fighting the last of my kind, I will do what I must. Even if it means ending my species forever."

"Why would… I do not understand."

"My people are the ones that started the extinction war. Inside, I will uncover the sins of my people. Perhaps I will be confronted with my own sins. If, after all of that, I must kill the last of my kin, I would next take my own life. Rid the world once and for all of the threat of my people who have caused so much hurt and harm."

"Taritie, you are not a threat. The only reason I and Myriusha lived as long as we did is because of you."

"You do not know everything about me, Tyrnol. I may have lived in an age of peace, but as I told you once before, I am not a healer."

CHAPTER FIVE: GATE

The capital gates stand like a threshold to a different realm. On the exterior, ominous clouds cling to the city's sloping walls, but within, the sun bathes the city in a radiant glow. The gates, a portal to a new world, beckon with their grandeur: colossal hinge doors, a bridge adorned with lush greenery, and towering golden statues, their arms outstretched in welcome.

"Incredible. No painting I've ever laid eyes on could capture the beauty of the Shappalan capital." Salie's jaw drops as she gazes through the gates. Then noticing the gate itself, she begins to study the intricate engravings chiseled on their surface.

Taritie, though not as captivated by the city, can't help but find her enthusiasm endearing. There is a warm and fuzzy feeling hearing and seeing her mesmerized and awe-stricken over his people that most would grind their teeth at. He sees her write down questions in her journal.

Realizing this could be a chance for him to show off a little, he says, "The capital has numerous different quarters for numerous species. The outermost circle is the agricultural district, the third circle is financial, the second circle is the high-born district, and the final and last circle is the royal district. There is also the undercity, which is its own separate entity from the upper city. The undercity has its own divisions and will be the safest and most direct route to the command center located in the royal district."

Salie hums and scribbles in glee. She is enthralled by what Taritie says and takes vigorous notes, trying to retain everything. Ryonis does not look interested, while Ashanna intentionally ignores the conversation.

Taritie looks at each of them and grumbles to himself. "Wonderful. I did not want children, but now I have three."

For some reason, that comment sparks Ashanna to life, "What was that?"

"I said, stay close to me and keep your eyes open."

Ashanna cringes at his words, "What do you have that all the people who went with my father did not?" Taritie pauses for a moment, seeing the resentment in her eyes. To Ashanna, it is clear that no matter what Taritie may say, it is going to make him the enemy.

"You are right. I do not have numbers on my side, but what I do have is foreknowledge and experience." Taritie, trying to defend himself only irritates Ashanna more. With a sigh, he pulls out his mother's necklace.

"I am sorry Ashanna. You did not choose to be here." Taritie reaches out and hands Ashanna his mother's necklace.

"This necklace? I thought I left this at the house." Ashanna runs her fingers across the smooth shield of the crest pendant. Taritie feels a strange sensation of a pair of eyes now turning their attention to him. As if the pendant has garnished the attention of some onlooker that Taritie cannot see.

"My mother gave me that pendant to remember her. I would clutch it anytime I felt alone. I would ask for you to continue to keep it safe for me." Ashanna's attitude softens. Her eyes become melancholy similar to how Taritie would become when holding that necklace.

Ashanna, as if realizing that she should be angry, stores the pendant and mutters to herself as she falls behind the group. Ryonis falls back with her. "So, uh... what do you think of the inside of the ruined capital?"

Ashanna looks up to Ryonis, who is wearing an unconvincing smile. Her first instinct is to brush him off, but she fights against her hurt. "I do not know, honestly; my father told me about the undercity when he was trapped there. He said it was unlike anything he had ever seen. I would not mind seeing it for myself as long as we do not die there."

"I will be excited when we get to see it, then. The place I

hope to see in the city is the Selestia quarter. I want to see what it may have been like for my people when they were living here."

"Now that you mention it, I would also like to see the Feylin quarter. Having all the races of Feylin in the same city must have been interesting. All the Feylin have since divided themselves based on color and powers."

Ashanna and Ryonis continue discussing and even start laughing. Taritie allows himself to relax, seeing her smile again. She seems to be under the most stress out of all of them. With Ryonis watching out for her, Taritie is determined to avoid repeating the mistake of the last expedition group; he returns his focus to what is around him. To his dismay, everything is dead quiet. Birds fly in the sky, large creatures up above and around them, and there is the occasional running small creature, nothing that could wipe out a large expedition force. It must be true that they are waiting somewhere ahead and lingering in some shadow or alley to jump out. For the moment, the highway here may be the safest spot in the capital.

Salie begins hugging Taritie's side, trying to get his attention. "This place is marvelous. My father devoted his life to the study of the ancient Big Three nations, and now I am inside the ruined capital itself. If only my father could see me now."

Taritie notices something strange about the giant flying creatures. One of them does not look like the others. He is not certain, yet the feeling of eyes watching him could be that creature. Taritie keeps his eyes on it and humors Salie simultaneously. "What do you hope to find in here?"

"The crown jewel of the ruined capital, of course. The reason that drew a thousand people to want to enter here and the reason still more will attempt it. The solution to every living person's problem: immortality."

Taritie realizes the odd one out in the sky is slowly descending. Like a gargoyle, it perches on a nearby tower overlooking the bridge ahead. Looking at the bridge, it would be an exceptional ambush point.

Taritie looks over at Salie and realizes she is waiting for his response, but he is at a loss for words. She calls him out, "You were not listening, were you?"

Taritie stares off into the distance, furrowing his brow and trying to remember. "No, I was listening. You were talking about the cure for mortality."

Salie smiles and remarks, "So, you were listening while you were staring off into space."

Taritie fights back a laugh. The last thing he is doing is letting himself become distracted in this city. "I was not ignoring you, I swear. I am a little lost in how to respond, though. Obtaining immortality is certainly a lofty goal. I imagine a professor would prefer to study the city instead of robbing it."

"You are mocking me."

"I am not mocking you; I am being serious. Why immortality?"

"The answer is simple: why study for a little while and create research on limited knowledge versus obtain immortality and be able to have all the time in the world to learn as much as possible?" Salie's orange eyes glow with a gleam of desire. It is clear her weakness is discovery. "My father spent his whole life piecing together knowledge, only for him to pass it down to me. One day, I will have to die and pass on my knowledge to someone else. So many things get lost in passing that knowledge down. Think of the advances we could make if we could keep working forever."

"You have put a lot of thought into this, it seems."

"I am not stupid, Taritie; I can see you are patronizing me. You treat everyone almost the same way. Your eyes look as if they are pained and bored when talking to anyone. You have this false smile and pretend you are present, but in reality, there is nothing that can keep your attention for longer than a breath. You are just like my father."

"Okay, I confess I was not listening."

"I knew you were not listening. Your eyes are off in your own world."

"I am trying to keep us alive." Salie rolls her eyes and stomps ahead by herself. Taritie shakes his head in utter bewilderment. Why can she not understand that he has concerns other than her when they are in this city?

At the foot of the bridge, Taritie takes a deep breath, knowing that whatever is about to happen is going to happen fast. However, he is not prepared for Ryonis interrupting his thoughts and tapping his shoulder. Taritie turns around and sees that Ryonis has his technician book in hand. "Taritie, there is someone behind us."

Taritie turns around and sees that there is indeed someone behind them—someone who has been trailing slowly behind for some time. The moment Ashanna's eyes connect with the figure, she starts running to him. "Father? What is he doing here?"

Behind Tyrnol, a large group of riders storm past the gate. A cacophony of hoofbeats echoes and bounces off the domed walls and sounds like a possessed roar. The riders are on what seems to be raven steeds. The armor of the group is specialized but hails from the province of Nocturna. Many of the riders already have weapons brandished and will soon overtake Tyrnol.

His words are frantic, but Taritie can already guess what Tyrnol is saying. "Run!"

Knowing they need to act swiftly, Taritie orders, "Ashanna, get back here." Taritie's words fall on deaf ears. Ashanna continues to run after her father. Feeling in his soul that chaos is about to strike, he turns toward Ryonis, grabbing his shoulders. "I am going after Ashanna. Whatever you do, do not cross that bridge. Find a way down to the river and a way to cross it or go down it. You control ice; freeze the whole river if you have to. Just make sure to get everyone safe." Taritie gives a glance at Salie. Taritie lets out an irritated sigh. He thinks to himself that if he had not been distracted, he might have noticed Tyrnol earlier. "The same goes for you. You are the oldest, so act it, Salie."

Ryonis realizes how quickly the raven steeds are approaching. "Taritie, we cannot escape them. We should stand our ground."

"Trust me, Ryonis."

In Taritie's head, he recalls the words he explained to Ryonis and Ashanna when they asked him about the Shappalans. The Feylin have energy veins that flow through them, allowing them unique access to energy both inside and outside their bodies. Selestia has the power to control and manifest elements at will. Lastly, the Shappalans, the third of the great races, have the astounding ability to influence anatomy in a way unlike any other. This ability could be as complex as a complete shapeshift to something as simple as strengthening the muscles in the legs to run faster and more robustly than what is ordinarily possible.

Taritie strengthens his legs and darts after Ashanna. Wearing the armor that he usually wears, the speed at which Taritie is running must have looked supernatural. Like the legends of old, in which God would give strength to men. He would typically never have used his shapeshifting for any reason. Ashanna was the exception to that rule; anonymity be damned.

Taritie slides in front of Ashanna, tackling her waist and sliding her onto his shoulder before spinning back around without losing his momentum. Ashanna screams and struggles in his grasp. Taritie turns his head to see Tyrnol leaning on his cane with a face that looks blurry from this distance. Taritie subconsciously enhances his eyes to see further. He sees the details of Tyrnol's face and can read the soundless words coming from his lips, "Thank you." The riders charge past Tyrnol. Ignoring the old man and keeping their sights solely on Taritie.

In front of him, he spies Salie and Ryonis. He sees a rope tied to the side of the bridge, and Ryonis is already lowering Salie down. Taritie drops Ashanna next to Ryonis. Looking back, he sees the knights fast approaching. Ryonis tries to get Ashanna tied and able to be lowered down, but she is fighting him and sobbing profusely. Taritie reaches out his hand to Ashanna. He applies a little pressure to her neck. He sends forth a little of his power into her. He reaches into her brain and commands her to sleep. When Taritie lets go, Ashanna lets out a few more cries before her eyes close, and she falls limp to the ground.

Taritie places his hand on Ryonis' shoulder. "Tie a rope to yourself, and you will go down next to Ashanna. You will protect Salie and Ashanna with your dying breath, and your goal will be the same as before. Make it to the command center of this ruined capital. It will be inside the castle-looking building in the center of the royal district."

Ryonis' eyes widen, and his face is clearly written with worry. "Are you leaving us?"

"Hopefully not. I will draw the riders onto the bridge and then throw myself into the river."

"That river leads to a waterfall; how will you survive?"

"I am sure it's not that bad of a fall. On the other hand, you need time to get her down, and I can give that to you." Taritie places his right hand up toward his head and gently away from him. The gesture is one of goodwill that his thoughts and mind will be with Ryonis no matter where he goes. It also expresses a hope that they will meet again.

"Be safe, Master." Taritie notices that this is the first time that Ryonis has recognized Taritie as his master. His words warm the warrior's heart.

"If I am able, I will see you at the foot of the waterfall." With that goodbye and the warmth in his chest, Taritie leaps onto the bridge and starts running for the other side. It is not lost to his eyes that the moment his feet pass the midway point of the bridge, the large, winged creatures start flying for the bridge. Taritie stops now, seeing the creatures flying for him. His eyes drift one last time to Ryonis. He has Ashanna in his lap and begins propelling her down to the ground.

"No more hesitation." Taritie positions himself at the threshold before the bridge. He takes his helmet, which had been tied to his waist up to this point, and fastens it to his head. While he attaches it, footsteps become louder—a wall of black steeds with a small fragment of their ranks splintering after the propelling children.

The eyes of the steeds are dark red jewels, shining with an animalistic wrath. Feathers fly from their coats from the beating of the boots of their masters. Their breath is spewing smoke in the frigid air of the fall morning. Within a moment, they would break upon Taritie, their bodies slamming against him and their feet trampling him as blades reach down and skewer him.

Taritie lowers the visor of his helmet. He throws away the sheath to his blade and readies to strike the feet of the lead horse in front of him. He enhances his whole body. His muscles begin to expand and tighten. The energy and heat produced by the expansion send a light steam rolling from his skin. With all of his strength poured into this stand, knowing it will not be enough, he resolves himself to face this enemy.

The horse wall comes within a breath of him. Taritie prepares to strike, but a quake in the ground causes him to stumble. Behind him, a behemoth of a bird perches on the bridge. The creature, having six wings of decreasing size, lets out a high-pitched screech that makes him raise his hands to his head, yet his helmet blocks him from covering his ears.

The horse wall stops in its place, and the creatures become erratic and start throwing their riders. One rider remains on his horse and attempts to turn and flee, though a man with wings swoops from the sky and tackles the rider. The man, with a brilliant shining spear, impales the soldier. The winged man begins slaughtering the downed riders. His movements are elegant and flowing like his body is a stream that flows with a current that only he can see.

Two of the riders manage to remount and dart away. The winged man does not give chase but watches as they flee. Soon, a shadow overtakes them, and a second large bird swoops down and picks up the riders and their horses. The bird takes them up into the sky and then releases them. They plummet to the ground and move no more.

The winged man turns to Taritie with his spear extended. His body is covered in the blood of the riders. Within a heartbeat, Taritie recognizes him as the immortal whom he feared would be here. This winged man is someone of years beyond counting. He knows this from his long, faded gray hair and the wings on his back that must have taken centuries to manifest naturally, and he knows he is ancient by his soulless silver eyes that make him look like a doll when put on his young face.

The winged man leaps into the air and, with a flap of his wings, glides in front of Taritie. Growing defensive, Taritie tightens his stance but is unsure of his ability to fight this man. The ancient rider is muscular, covered in scars, and a little bit taller than Taritie. He approaches Taritie, but suddenly, his eyes become warm. Taritie feels an unnatural calm rest on his soul. The winged man reaches out his arms and grasps Taritie in a warm embrace. Like a father after seeing his child return home. The grip around Taritie tightens, and the ancient immortal begins to cry. Taritie's mind begins to panic, and thoughts flood into his head without end.

Every ounce of logic within Taritie's head tells him this is the enemy. He begins to reason in his head, "He is a remnant of the great war. He released monsters and turned machines against anyone who entered. He killed so many people who were only curious about the city, and yet why? Why am I happy?"

The rider steps back, and his soulless eyes have a new gleam. He greets Taritie, "I thought I was alone. I opened my eyes and awoke in these ruins, believing that I was the only one left. You do not know how happy it makes me to see that I was wrong."

Taritie wants to ask so many questions. There are things that must be answered. Despite his worries, more sentimental emotions overwhelm him. "I know what that feels like."

He notices the blood that has stained him by hugging the man. The blood now clings to his armor and on his hands, where he reciprocated the man's embrace. He looks past the winged man and toward the piles of bodies that small creatures have already gathered around to feast on.

The winged man turns around and lets out a light chuckle. "Look how eager the city reacts to their remains. The taste of flesh has been withheld from the city for far too long."

A sharp, uncomfortable pang hits Taritie's chest. "Who are you?"

"Ah, how rude of me! I have not introduced myself. Let me fly you to the capital, and I will explain myself on the way there."

"No, I cannot leave. There are those waiting on me. I need to protect them."

"Other Shappalans?"

"No, they are children of Selestia and Feylin that have

been thrust into my care."

"Your pets can wait; our people's future is by far more pressing." Taritie feels a sensation like a splinter shoved deep into his cranium. This is confirmation of the fears that he has been holding on to.

Without allowing Taritie to speak against him, the winged man spins Taritie around and carries him into the sky.

The winged man then asks, "I can tell by the way you were walking that you are not all too familiar with the capital, are you?"

Taritie feels aggravated by the disrespect. He tries to shake out of the winged man's grip but without any success. In an irritated tone, Taritie replies, "No, I have visited it only twice before."

"Good. Then I, Mylos, will give you a tour of areas you have never seen. Wonders which were never allowed to be known by anyone other than those of the inner court."

"What? Why would you show me the secrets of the capital? That honor is only given to the high-born. You do not even know who I am."

"You make an excellent point. What is your name?"

Taritie hesitates. He should not trust this man with his identity. However, the past is catching up with him, and the more he keeps it inside himself, the more unstable he becomes.

If he continues to shoulder all the burdens of the past alone, he will fall apart. Here is someone that he can not only confide in but who would understand his struggles. Perhaps using this man to stabilize his own mind could inversely help Mylos.

Taritie takes a deep breath, pausing to collect himself. "I am Taritie, an engineer and scientist contracted to help with the Selestia time freeze project."

"It is only fair that I introduce myself now that I am acquainted with you. I was the first-seat war admiral and military advisor to the royal council. I governed over the Black Diamond Fleet and overseer to the Selestia war front." Mylos, after introducing himself, starts chuckling, "I am quite familiar with you, Taritie. Now it makes sense why you survived all this time."

"You know me?"

"Every Shappalan during the war knows you, the only one of our kind to be allowed into that foolish project. You likely have no idea how many people held out hope for that project to succeed and for it to stop the inevitable war. How quickly though hope shifts to regret in hindsight."

"Regret?"

"It is not important. The war happened, and now we live with the consequences. All that matters now is we are together. From our unity will spawn a new age for not just this world but this galaxy." Mylos lands at the foot of the great citadel that is the center of the ruined capital.

Taritie can feel something off in his soul. He has lived a long life and has seen every kind of person there is. He has known betrayal and knows those who would do harm before they even could commit the act. He has safeguarded his heart with his acute logic and sensibility. His intuition and experiences with people have always informed him before a storm hit, and it has never led him astray. But, for the first time in his life, he is fighting against his intuition. His mind weighs the sins that he may commit versus the sting of loneliness he has known. After weighing them, Taritie's eyes brighten, and he smiles and feels giddy. He has made his choice, and the worry drains from every pore. For the first time since his childhood, his face takes on a young expression and character that matches his complexion.

Ryonis repels down the rope. His boots hit the ground with a thud, and he moves quickly to untie the ropes. Salie, who was waiting at the bottom, rushes to assist as shouting echoes from above them.

Salie searches for Taritie. "Where is Taritie? Was he not right behind you?"

Ryonis looks up to the bridge. "You better meet us at the bottom." Shouting echoes down as knights find the rope and begin to repel down. "I will explain later. Right now, we need to move."

Salie starts running away, but Ryonis trips and nearly faceplants into the ground. He looks down and notices a rope still tied to his leg. Ryonis struggles furiously with the rope around him. "Help me get out of this; it is not coming apart."

Salie looks over and sees Ryonis struggling. His hands are shaking, and he keeps fumbling as he struggles to untie it. Salie lets out a sigh, takes one of Ryonis' knives, cuts the rope, and then looks up at him, flustered. "You just told me we need to move. Calm down for a moment and think."

Salies turns back around while Ryonis hoists Ashanna onto his back. He takes off down the sidewalk bordering the river. "Do you have to make everyone feel horrible?"

"No, it is just hard being surrounded by people who think slower than me."

"Think slower? You are older than me, and Taritie is certainly smarter, but you still treat him like refuse."

"It is not my fault you are younger. When I was your age, my father never simplified his words. He told me to catch up and suck it up."

"I'm sorry your father was a jerk, but do you have to take it out on us?"

"I love my father. What are you babbling about?"

"You are insufferable! I cannot believe I thought you were a princess when we first met. Now I realize you were a brat, just not the royal kind."

"Nice comeback. Do you think you can put that energy into running, though?"

Close on their heels, the raven-steed knights hit the ground. They gain on Ryonis, but his movements are slow due to Ashanna's weight. The enemy lifts their blades and aims for his back. Ryonis pulls his book with his offhand. He flips to a random page. He looks down, sees an ice shield, and turns to use it. A knight hurls a spear toward Ryonis and is caught by the ice shield. The spear nearly penetrated the shield, its tip a breath away from Ryonis' nose. Ryonis bursts the shield, sending the spear flying back and shards of ice at the approaching knights.

Ryonis goes back to flipping through the pages until he arrives at the cold wind. With a smile, he sends forth the icy blast toward his enemies. Their movements are slow, but something is off from all the other times he has used it. The freezing is slow, and the knights are still moving.

Salie rushes beside Ryonis and pulls him to start running

again. "Those are the elite troops of Nocturna. They carry charms to dull the effects of all Selestia powers." A knight manages to reach out and grab Ryonis, but Salie, using her satchel, knocks the slowed knight in the head, and he reels back.

Salie looks down at her bag and whimpers. "If that broke my compass or any of my tools, I am going to make those knights pay for the repairs."

"You are not serious, are you?"

Salie cocks a judgmental glance at Ryonis. "Yes, obviously, I plan on inviting them over for tea as well."

The two enter an underpass that leads into the undercity. The sidewalk turns to steps bordering a waterfall that has quite a nasty drop. The knights once more catch up to them. Ryonis looks back and lets out a whine of frustration. His breath is ragged, his hair has turned black again, and he needs a rest. He desperately thinks of some way to stop them, but his mind keeps coming up with useless answers. Being distracted, he nearly trips on the stairs and almost drops Ashanna. He looks over the side and sees a long and horrible fall. That is when a moment of clarity arises in Ryonis. An idea that may buy him the time he needs.

Ryonis sets Ashanna down, then opens his book and sends out the last lingering breaths of his power. An incredible force of icy wind is directed not at his enemy but at the steps.

The damp stone steps begin freezing over and are covered with a thick layer of ice.

One of the knights tests the ice with his iron foot and nearly falls off the side. His comrades grab him and steady him. Stepping away from the ice, the enemy knights stand next to each other, refusing to go forward. They look over the railless edge to the long drop-down and back at the ice. Ryonis hears them begin cursing in their tongues. He almost wishes he spoke their language to understand their frustration and enjoy it a little more.

Salie comes behind Ryonis and waves at the powerless enemies. "I cannot believe that actually worked."

Ryonis gently picks up Ashanna. "Let's gain some ground before that ice melts."

Salie, with a toothy grin, says, "Gladly, let's leave these morons in the dust."

CHAPTER SIX: UNDERGROUND

The undercity of the ruined capital, a chasm unparalleled with great stone pillars reaching up to the ceiling, scattered ancient stone ruins, mushrooms the size of ancient trees, large floating orange and blue orbs radiating light, crystal mountains and ravines, lush plant life, intimidating creatures; each aspect of this place is alien to Ryonis. The domain seems alive in a way, unlike the surface city. This feeling compounds as Ryonis is the first off the stairs carrying Ashanna, and his footsteps off the path cause a reaction. The ground comes alive with a glowing blue light, acting like a nervous system. The light appears to run away like it is sending signals around the chasm. Salie, behind Ryonis, seems breathless, looking around and trying to comprehend the vastness and beauty of the land. She stares up at the ceiling covered in blue and white crystals resembling the galaxy itself.

Salie falls to her knees. "In all my life, I have never seen anything so beautiful."

Ryonis could see the chasm from the stairs, but with the adrenaline and the present danger, there was no time to appreciate it. Now, at the bottom of the stairs, with the sound of the river roaring, the strange creatures echoing their sounds and cries, and all of the splendor of this land on display, it is hard not to become entranced and hypnotized by the abundance of supernatural sights—so much so that he did not notice Ashanna waking up.

Ashanna, with eyes wide open and mouth slightly ajar, stares at Ryonis and wonders if this is what her father felt when he first saw the mystical beauty of the undercity. Thinking of her father and the dangers he talked of, she remembers that even roses have thorns and shakes Ryonis from his trance as she speaks softly, "Would you mind lowering me down?"

Ryonis starts at the sound of her voice but squats down, allowing Ashanna to gently get off his back. He notices her soft expression and sad eyes. He asks, "Are you doing okay?"

Ashanna looks up at the ceiling and around at the undercity around them. Her chest feels sour, and her eyes are watering, yet she cannot help but look in wonder. She is close to tears when she recenters herself and notices Taritie is missing. With her heart beating a little faster, she asks Ryonis, "Where is Taritie? Why is he not with us?"

"He stayed behind to buy us time. He told me he would leap into the waterfall and meet us here, but I do not think so. That seems asinine, even for him. In truth, I do not know where he is now." Ryonis looks down in defeat and points to the light that peaks over the waterfall. It is impossible to see the bridge from where they are standing. "There is hope, though. I did see a great number of the Nocturna knights floating down the river. There is a chance he pulled off a miracle and is heading to the command room right now. If that is the case, we must meet him."

Ashanna sees the knights on the staircase beating at the frozen stairs, and she feels her heart start to beat faster. Anger mixed with fear kicks in, and she finds herself grinding her teeth and shivering. She looks to Ryonis. "We need to hurry to that command room. If any of the knights survived that fall, I do not want them beating us there."

Ryonis scoffs and looks up at the knights working so hard to try and break his ice. He glances down at the river where bodies and supplies float down. "Some of the knights who fell down the waterfall made it to shore, but the knights on those stairs are going to be stuck for a while. I froze half that staircase while walking down. Those that fell down the falls... well, these knights may be tough foes, but I doubt many, if any, survived that fall."

Ashanna finally pieces it together and inquires, "Wait, you fought off the knights and carried me all this way?"

"I had no choice."

"You look exhausted, and I have been nothing but a burden. I must ask your forgiveness, Ryonis."

Ryonis scoffs. "No, I will not give you my forgiveness because you have done nothing wrong. Do you honestly think that if our roles were reversed, I would have done anything different?" Ryonis grabs Ashanna's hand and raises it as he stares into her eyes. "I was not there to protect my family. I swear to you that if my father was in front of me and in danger, I would have run to him without any other thought in my mind. Just as what happened to you, I would have had to be dragged kicking and screaming."

Ashanna's eyes well up with tears, and she shuts them, rubs away the tears, and leans her head against Ryonis. She takes only a moment before collecting herself and stepping away. She stands up straighter, looking more confident. "Thank you, Ryonis, for carrying me and for your words.

Ryonis shakes his head. "I recently lost my parents. I do not blame you for losing your cool. I… no…" Ryonis fights back the familiar melancholy. "You still have hope. Your father is alive, I can feel it."

Ashanna starts fidgeting with her hands and her cheeks

turn red. Her eyes seem to meet Ryonis' in a way that is different from before. She quickly glances away. "You bought us time, and I am glad about that, but do you think we can start heading to the command room right now?"

Ashanna sees a little of the exhaustion that bleeds out from Ryonis, unaware of the true extent. Ryonis bites the inside of his lip, trying not to show weakness. His insides are like a cloud on a hot desert day. All that is left inside of him is being pulled out, and sooner rather than later, he will be unable to stand.

With a smile, Ryonis gives her a nod and walks over to Salie, who is busy scooping up some of the dirt and glowing grass and placing them into glass jars. He says, "We need to get moving and gain some distance from those knights before we make camp. Are you able to go a little further?"

Salie looks up, her eyes glowing. "You are wondering if I want to go deeper into this wonderland? Should that not be obvious?" Salie looks around like a child walking into a bakery for the first time. "If we can, I would like to examine the ruins, see if the ancient writings match my knowledge of their language, and study some local wildlife."

Ashanna remembers what her father told her. "We want to be careful of beasts and machines. My father mentioned that they became hostile the moment they lay eyes on you. We may want to keep away from large creatures."

Ryonis, trying to seem energetic, replies, "That is reasonable. Taritie may not be with us, but I know we can survive if we work together."

Salie gives him a strange look. "You do not sound even remotely convinced of what you just said. From what I have seen, especially in the forest leaving Solis, you are like his son. Do you even know how to act when he is not holding your hand?"

Ryonis sighs. "Salie, I thought we had a moment on the staircase."

"Baby steps, Ryonis." Salie turns her head and smirks when he cannot see her face.

Ashanna leads the way, and Ryonis trails next to Salie. Thankfully, her constantly distracted nature sets the perfect pace for Ryonis. Together, they explore the undercity, following a stone path leading deeper in and not straying too far. Salie occasionally leaves the group to waste time oggling over some monolith or ruin covered in ancient texts. Machines would often pass by, but they seemed harmless as long as they did not spot them. Most of the machines look to be taking care of fauna, planting, and taking care of what looks to be some farm or some other processes that are beyond what any of them can understand. The only major problem is keeping track of time.

Ryonis feels his body shaking but continues to press on,

trying to act tough. Salie and Ashanna are absorbed by their concerns, and Ryonis himself does not want to make them worry. Typically, Selestia technicians train their endurance to be more effective technicians and, when depleted, relax for one to two days to recover their energy. However, Rynonis understands that even if they were to get a break, he would be back up and at it again within a few hours. Ashanna is hurting in her own way, and Ryonis would love to help her if he was not so exhausted.

Salie looks back and notices how Ryonis is starting to sway back and forth. His forehead is covered in sweat, and his eyes look unfocused. "Are you alright? You look ready to collapse."

Ryonis notices everyone stopping to stare at him, and he takes this time to look for a place to sit down. He notices a large tree with numerous vine-like branches that resemble a lush head of hair. Ryonis moves aside the vines, sees the trunk of the tree, and sits down with his back propped against it. Ryonis breathes rapidly. Through the breaths, he assures, "I am fine, I just need a little rest, and I will be back up in no time."

Ashanna looks at him and knows the signs well. She remembers her training and understands just as well as him what it means to be out of energy. The way one's body feels deprived of necessary nourishment; it is similar to sickness, and it is dangerous if ignored. Ashanna sighs and tells Salie, "We are making camp here tonight. I will make a fire. If you start setting things out, we can look for food together. I know how to fish, and I know you should be able to gather some plants. I trust you more than any of us to find something edible."

Salie nods nervously. "I will do what I can, but all of this is new to me."

Ryonis continues to breathe heavily while Ashanna and Salie do all of the work. Ryonis feels annoyed and helpless. He rises, and his body forces him back down. He remembers this feeling well. The feeling of a weight on his stomach and the pains of breathing. It took him three days to recover from this the previous time, and he doubts that he even has a single night to recover. What makes it worse is that Ryonis feels he has himself to blame. He should have recovered most of his strength in the week it took to get to the ruined capital. Too much weighed on his mind back then for him to get any proper rest. Now, he is rendered utterly useless because of a little bit of exertion. Ryonis slams his fist into the ground, and it causes a reverberation of blue light.

Ryonis curses under his breath. "I need to get up. Move legs."

Ashanna approaches Ryonis and lays her hand on him. "Stop worrying. You carried me. Let me help you now. All you need to do is rest."

"I do not like being useless. I do not like asking for help either."

"You trust Taritie to help you. Trust in me." With those words, Ryonis resigns himself against the tree. Ashanna leaves and starts working to unpack. She puts what little wood she can find in the center of the campsite.

Ashanna and Salie wander off to gather food once they finish setting up the campsite. Ryonis, unable to move, stays under the tree a few steps away from the unlit campfire. After a moment, he hears the sound of rustling foliage. He prepares to see Ashanna or Salie returning to camp, but the figure that appears is not at all who he expects.

A large woman steps into the middle of the makeshift camp. On her body is midnight black metal armor with glowing golden designs. The armor is similar to that of a knight, but there are differences in the design, and the emblem on her black and gold dress-like cloth surcoat that hangs over her armor is foreign to him. Unlike Solis' armor, this armor was much more decorative than functional. Her movements make Ryonis think the armor itself must be light, especially considering her footsteps do not make the typical clinking sound that Ryonis is used to. Instead, that sound is altogether absent. Her armor did emanate a sound, a sound that can only be described as the metal smoothly gliding and comfortably moving like joints in a body. Ryonis' eyes trail to her gauntlets, where the woman clutches a blade that seems comical in size. Taritie is undoubtedly shorter than this woman, but his longsword would have to be at least half the size of this behemoth of a knight's greatsword. She wore a seamless black helm with more golden details. The woman examines the unlit campfire and the supplies dropped and left by Salie. The woman scans the area and walks over to the tree, but does not see him behind the vines. She looks perpendicular to where he lies and is close enough that with the orange glow of a nearby crystal, he can make out golden-ringed eyes, eyes that look oddly familiar to Taritie's. Another strange sight is under that helm. He sees a hint of brown hair sprinkled with gold dust under the visor.

The figure whips around and startles Ryonis. Her attention is not on him, however, but drawn to another figure behind her. This inhuman figure is an entirely unknown creature to him. It is covered in grey and black hair, similar to fur, with a large mane on its head that falls to the ground. The seven-foot-tall creature with lengthened shins and ankles and a head similar to a canine with light blue eyes walks closer into the light. The beast sports similar black armor, but this creature's armor does not have all the golden details and looks well-worn.

The large creature rubs its nose and sniffles. "Lady Hannia, it seems the pests are not here at the moment. I did spot intruders down by the river, though."

Hannia ridicules, "Lyora, this is the second time you have led me to an empty camp. When is your nose going to start working again?"

Lyora does not seem phased by Hannia's remark and answers, "Forgive me, my lady. The time-freezing process had some sort of negative effect on my nose. I am sure it will be back to normal in no time."

"It does not matter. From the few we have interrogated, it does not seem these creatures have any information on my prey." Hannia walks over and bends down next to a satchel on the ground. "What is your opinion on this new age, Lyora?"

"It is primitive, similar to my people when the Shappalans first found us on our home world."

"Well, yes, but that is not what I was talking about." Hannia picks up Salie's book and starts flipping through it. "I guess I did not word myself very well."

"Do not say that, my lady, it is my fault for being ignorant."

"Stop groveling. I understand you were put in my service right before the final siege, but I want a servant, not a slave. That means being polite, not pretending you have to cater to my every whim."

"Forgive me, my lady. I will aim to become better and be

able to satisfy you in any way you desire."

"You are making it worse, Lyora." Hannia raises her hand to her helm and takes it off. Her long hair flows freely and falls down her back. Ryonis cannot help but blush a little, seeing her beautiful face. "Perhaps I phrased it worse before. How do I phrase it better? My last servant, Samala, was more than a servant. She was a friend of mine. I have had plenty of lovers and servants but few friends. Do you not understand?"

"I do not understand, my lady. If you would like, though, I may treat you more formally if you so wish me to."

"I figured Samala was joking when she said she was more carefree compared to the rest of her people." Hannia moves over to the small campfire and places her sword in the middle of it. She presses down on a circular metal piece that slides into the shaft, and the sword's blade lights up with a glow, and the wood ignites into flames. She releases the metal piece, and the light stops glowing as the flames continue to engulf the wood.

"Anyway, what I was saying before I got sidetracked, people here have a purpose. Look at this," she picks up Salie's book again. "This is a simple and easy-to-understand language, but I can ascertain the qualities of the writer based on this script. That was unknown to my people. It was considered primitive writing, but the writing is beautiful. This writer must have an uncanny sense of wonder and curiosity. I would give much to feel that again."

"What importance does wonder have? They can dream all they wish but it will not give them power or extend their lives beyond the dust. They should be subjugated and adopted into the fold like my people were."

"Good Architect above; that just makes me feel awful inside, Lyora." Hannia looks at the book closer to the fire, and the fire reaches out and burns her, to her surprise. She looks in wonder at the strange sensation and points out, "The reversal of immortality has even affected me. How am I any different from these people?"

"They are easy to kill, my lady, and you are not."

"Yes, but the question that is most on my mind is, am I the only one of my kind left aside from that weasel in the citadel?" Hannia flips a page and continues reading. "If I am, should I not make peace with these creatures as my people did before the war? I think the war has become all I know, and maybe I should consider my life beyond it."

"What of it, my lady, if you and the master in the citadel are all that is left, should you not make peace with him in an effort to produce the next generation of Shappalan?"

"You make me sound so animalistic." Lyora seems to take minor offense to the comment and blinks her eyes a few times in silence before Hannia notices, "I do not mean to offend, of course."

"I have already moved on, my lady. What is important is the continuation of your species. If there were anyone left of my people, that is what I would seek."

"That weasel of a man is a monster. Not only that, but he is about seven thousand years older than I." Hannia closes the book and reaches her hand out into the fire. The fire starts to burn her, and Lyora quickly runs over and grabs her hand out of the flames. "After he fired the weapon that made all species throughout the galaxy mortal again, he gloated while watching the poisoned atmospheres of countless worlds kill billions. What bothers me most is that I still do not know what secret he used to bypass the effects of his own weapon. Back to the point, I could never imagine any reality where I lay with such a sick, twisted, empty, selfish—"

"I understand, my lady, forgive me for bringing it up."

"You interrupted me."

"Sorry, my lady, what discipline fits my rudeness?"

"Discipline? I almost want to give you a treat. I did not think you had it in you, to be honest." Hannia puts the book back in the satchel, stands up, and stretches. Lyora takes out a strange bottle filled with liquid, and it spits out something onto Hannia's burn. The burn disappears in a moment.

Hannia continues, saying, "No, the fiend may not be my

prey, but he is just as worthy of death. He may not have started the war, but he ended it in a way that I can never forgive."

"What is our next move, my lady?"

"We will return to the citadel. I will kill the weasel, and then I will scour this world to see, perhaps, if he was not lying, that the traitor is still alive and immortal. It may take a thousand years to search this world, but that is nothing once I claim immortality from the dead body of the weasel."

"Which weasel are you referring to now, my lady?"

"Oh, forget it."

"Well, I will surely be dead before you finish, but may I suggest you think about finding some means to continue your people before you die? As your servant, it would be dishonorable of me if I did not think of your continuation. And please consider subjugating and educating these lesser creatures."

"I will think about it. Let us get going, I need to relieve some stress, and there is a certain immortal whom I wish to decapitate."

"My lady, two figures are approaching."

Ryonis is certain that she is talking about Salie and Ashanna. Ryonis begins to worry. These two are unknowns. If he watches while they kill Ashanna and Salie, he could never forgive himself.

"What would you have me do? I have already asked

numerous questions to the previous knights, and they know nothing of a Shappalan named Taritie." Ryonis' eyes go wide when she says his name. Ryonis knows that Taritie is a descendant of the Shappalans, but why would this lady know of him? She mentioned prey and traitor. Does that mean that Taritie is not just any Shappalan, but an immortal?

"My lady, please take your frustrations out on these two and spare Mylos. If you want to be my friend, this is my request."

"Goodness, you are persistent. I suppose you took my words about being more of an individual to heart. Even if you are only being individualistic for my service." Hannia stands up and pulls her blade from the fire. "Fine, but I am still killing the weasel if they do not satisfy me."

"I cannot complain, my lady. Thank you for recognizing my request." Lyora whisks her hand, and a purple portal appears. Lyora reaches her hand in and pulls out a black spear.

Ryonis starts shaking and trying to get up, but his body will not move. He tries to say something, but his voice is silent in fear. His heart beats a thousand miles per hour, but he does not know what to do. That is when, before he understands what is happening, a spear appears directly underneath his chin.

Looking up, Ryonis spies the inhuman lady with a predatory glare in her eyes. He can tell within a second she wants to kill him but does not make a move to do so. "My lady,

I have found another one. It seems he has been here the whole time. I only just a second ago heard his labored breathing."

Hannia jabs, "You must be sicker than I thought. I remember hearing you sniffle and rub your ears, but for you to not notice someone's breathing or even their heartbeat even though they were right next to us is truly pathetic."

"My lady, forgive my embarrassment. I am incapable of your defense. Should I pay with my life?"

Hannia looks bewildered at the request. "What? I am not going to tell you to kill yourself."

"This one looks sickly and not any pleasure for you. Should I end him swiftly?"

"That is fine, I have no use for him."

Ryonis' breath refuses to leave his lungs, and only one word comes out of his throat, "Taritie..." The two pause for a moment and look at him with serious expressions. Hannia leans down and examines Ryonis' face. Ryonis mutters, "I know Taritie."

Lyora goes silent and looks toward Hannia. Her face and demeanor change entirely. Hannia grabs Ryonis by the collar of his tunic and demands, "How do you know of him, and what does he look like? If you are lying, death would be a blessing."

"He is my master. He trained me and taught me everything I know."

"What does he look like?"

"He is wearing worn and beaten armor. He has black hair and golden eyes, and he is a few inches shorter than you." Hannia sets down Ryonis, ties his hands with rope, and hoists him up onto her back.

"Lyora, I will grab this one and return to the citadel. You will go and capture his friends. They must return to this camp. If they resist, you have my permission to hurt them, but not to kill them." Ryonis watches helplessly as Lyora gives a courteous bow.

"Understood, my lady, your wishes shall be done."

CHAPTER SEVEN: BEAST

Inside the undercity, time loses all meaning. There is no way of telling day from night aside from the small cracks in the ceiling where a waning golden light shines down. The light is not enough to illuminate the vast underground. Even with the glow and light from other sources, an eeriness perverses the surroundings which instills a sense of growing exhaustion upon Ashanna. This feeling is made manifest by the ever growing weight on her eyes, which is compounded by the heavy and pressing anxiety that grows like a resilient mold.

Near the river, Salie and Ashanna can look up and see the edges of the campsite they had set up. Their main focus is on their immediate surroundings, however. All along the river, there are signs of a significant battle between a few knights. Watching through the trees, some horrifying beasts are lingering with piercing green eyes. The bodies of the knights were mutilated and ripped to ribbons of flesh. Smaller animals carry away the bodies. Despite this gruesome scene, Salie and Ashanna do not depart.

Salie's eyes dart around with worry and dread. She begins to shake, but with some deep breaths, she keeps herself together. She holds a basket of berries and a few large purple fruits. "Should we head back to Ryonis? I know he is normally more than capable on his own, but should we have left him alone for this long? He can hardly move."

Ashanna, using her powers, creates a net that she casts to catch fish that swim and jump through the river in multitudes. Blood from the bodies upstream occasionally drifts by and clouds her view. She takes a small break after a cast. "Ryonis will be more than fine without us. If he is anything similar to me, he just needs a little rest and will be back up in no time."

Salie goes a little farther from the river, near a thicket with glowing berries. She grabs one and tastes it before putting more in her bag. "But right now, he is powerless if anyone came for him. He would not even be able to fight back in his state."

Ashanna unwraps a fish from her net, strings it through a rope, weaving the rope through the fish's mouth and past its gills. She drops it before returning to the river to catch another. "Do not forget he has combat experience, unlike either of us. I am certain he is trained to save a reserve of energy to ensure he can get out of harm's way if need be."

"What if he already used his reserve? After all, he froze all of those stairs and seemed exhausted before we even started walking around here. And I know he has not been sleeping well."

Ashanna is about to make another net but looks at the fish she caught and the fruit that Salie picked. "I suppose we can head back. This is probably enough for the three of us."

Salie stops, grabs her basket, and starts carrying it with two hands. "Thank you for listening, Ashanna. I am just worried."

"What worries me is you are older than me." Ashanna looks up, and Salie seems confused.

"What are you saying? I do not act older?"

"Nothing; I suppose you are just different." Ashanna wonders how this girl can be an adult. She is suggesting that Ashanna, a child, should make a final decision. The adults from the village would have immediately ordered they go back to Ryonis if they thought he could not handle being alone. Salie is only voicing her irritating opinion without invoking any action.

"I feel like you are insulting me, but I do not know what you are referencing."

"Forget it, I know we are all worried. How can we not be, in this place?" Ashanna's eyes dart to the gruesome scene, a rock toss away. She eventually sees a giant insect appear out of the trees and begin dragging away a body. Quickly looking away and refocusing on her task, Ashanna grabs the rope with the fish and waits for Salie to cross the river before starting the trek around and back up to the campsite. "What makes you so worried about him, anyway?"

"He and Taritie are my saviors. They came to my rescue despite being completely outnumbered. It was the most heroic thing I have ever witnessed."

"So, despite your rudeness to them, you think of them as heroes?" A weed of anxiety starts to take root within Ashanna. She feels a tightening in her chest, and she finds herself playing with her hands.

"Well, they saved me again today. Like a lamb, I feel so useless and helpless, but neither seem to hold it against me. A part of me felt guilty while we were running on the stairs. I should have been able to do something more. I have Selestia blood just as he does and have had some minor training. I could have done something, but I trusted him to do everything instead. I feel... indebted to Ryonis, I suppose."

"Is Ryonis not a bit young for you?"

Salie looks baffled by the accusation. She does not blush but is a little offended. "What do you think I am talking about Ashanna?"

Ashanna gets a little defensive. "Well, you talk of him like you are ready to fall at his feet."

"I do not talk like that. I suppose to your immature mind, it may seem like that." Salie starts to walk faster, trying to outpace Ashanna. "My worries for the child come from a desire for repayment."

Salie passes by Ashanna, and Ashanna realizes she may have gone a bit overboard by accusing her of fancying Ryonis. Picking up the pace, Ashanna catches up to her. "I am sorry. I did not mean to be abrupt."

Salie and Ashanna both slow down and look at each other. Salie sighs. "Ryonis is a child in my eyes, and it is embarrassing to have to rely on him. I know that is unfair to him, but it is true. I want to find some way to feel how I am… like what you said, older."

"Yes, I think that is understandable. I may have let my thoughts run too fast."

They walk silently for a few moments, and Salie thinks back to the conversation. Looking over at Ashanna, she suddenly starts to smile. "Wait, do you like Ryonis?"

Ashanna blushes and tries to act aloof. "Absolutely not; after all, boys are disgusting."

"This explains everything. Of course you were getting defensive. You are absolutely obsessed with him." Salie starts laughing rather loudly, and Ashanna tries to gesture for her to quiet down.

"I am not obsessed with him. I think he is attractive and capable." Ashanna's words fall on deaf ears. She hangs her head low while Salie laughs, and when she stops laughing, there is an ear-to-ear smile across her face. Ashanna's red cheeks only get redder. "This is not fair; you are making fun of me, and I have no defense."

"You do not need to be so embarrassed; it is cute. At your age, no one judges much who you fancy or not. It is not until you get a year or two older that your family starts trying to either marry you off or place high expectations on who can court you."

While Salie and Ashanna giggle and laugh, they do not notice a pair of eyes studying and examining them. It could also be because this feeling has been with them the entire time they have been in the undercity. There is always something out in the darkness.

The undercity, like a sentient creature, starts to awaken. The nearby lights begin to darken except for the blue and purple lights from the glowing plants, which become brighter. The large trees and shroom pillars start to sway and sound like whispering through the forest. The forest creatures stop what they are doing like machines and watch with curious eyes.

Salie and Ashanna stop talking when cool air blows upon them. They are almost at the camp, but a quiet ambience worse than a demented choir perverts the area. Following the quiet is a darkening that makes it difficult for them to see the path beneath their feet.

Salie pulls from her pocket a small wooden obelisk with carved writing. She focuses on one of the carvings, and wisps of flame appear in the air around her. The wisps illuminate pairs of eyes, staring at them through the trees.

Salie steps back, grabbing Ashanna's sleeve before realizing what she is doing and letting go. "Ashanna, the monsters have noticed us."

"Something is wrong; there is something different about how the monsters act. About the way the entire Undercity is acting."

"You make it sound like this place is alive."

"From what I have heard from Taritie and my father, I think this place is somewhat alive."

"What do we do?"

"They are not attacking, so let's try to make it to camp."

"Okay, I will follow you." Salie and Ashanna continue walking on the path, and the monsters' eyes follow them. They do not jump out and attack them even as their backs are turned away. Salie shudders. "It is almost like they are studying us."

Salie spots the camp first. She notices smoke coming from the fire and asks, "Did Ryonis somehow start the fire?"

Ashanna rushes underneath the tree, moves the tendrils

out of the way, and spies only barren soil and mushrooms. She informs Salie, "Ryonis is not under here. Check the tents?"

Salie moves to the tents and throws them open. She looks underneath the blankets and steps back, confused. Ashanna starts to look at the edges of the camp. They both continue to search, neither noticing the figure looming with a twisted, demented smile.

A cacophany begins to rise from the surrounding forest like cheering. Small creatures and insects start to make small, alarming noises that rise and grow with the light of nearby fauna. Soon, footsteps approach, and all the sounds slowly draw to a quiet and steady beat. More considerable footsteps from oversized creatures make a rhythm in the ground as they approach to watch. The sound of the gargantuan creatures approaching is like that of a quickening heartbeat.

Ashanna continues to look through the forest, and when she moves aside the leaves of a large bush, she sees the form of a creature she has never seen. The figure of a beast with a canid face without emotions other than a crooked smile leaning to the right. The person notices Ashanna and the face turns to her. Their unnatural eyes glow with a green shimmer. Their voice is low and monotone, with slight feminine cues. "Would you like to know where your tasty friend is?"

Ashanna's blood runs cold, and tears come to her eyes.

She finds her heart beating faster and the blood draining in her face. From the words of this demon, the fate she imagines of what has happened to Ryonis makes her quake and her sanity begins to waver. All of the haunting memories of her father being left behind return, and new images of Ryonis join them. While she is frozen with thoughts like a hurricane swirling inside her mind, the beast grabs her and leans closer, whispering, "Do not worry your heart. I, Lyora of the Lyciens, will take you to him."

Lyora, the arrogant beast, did not know she had made a mistake. She assumed Ashanna was frozen in fear. She used evidence of her tears and heart rate to support this. But Ashanna was not frozen. Instead, her mind was thinking faster and more keenly than ever before.

Ashanna could feel the threads of her sanity stretching and snapping. All of the restraints that kept her at bay were breaking. She remembers the words of her mother on how to restrain herself. The phrases she would chant to prevent herself from hurting anyone. But now, she has no reason to care who gets hurt. Ryonis is gone. Her mind reaffirms this to her repeatedly despite how hard she tries to deny it. This world has already taken so much from her, and what left does she have to show for it?

Lyora, in a more confident tone, whispers, "Come quietly,

and do not make me have to work too hard."

Ashanna gently pulls the stowed necklace and runs her fingers along it. She desperately tries to comfort herself, not realizing the diamonds in the crown are glowing red. "I should have listened to Salie. She knew something was wrong, and I did not listen. This is all my fault." Ashanna's mind starts to become manageable. Her thoughts start flowing to a pace she can keep up with, and they all tell her the same course of action. Demanding her to take this action.

She bites her lip to the point that blood spills into her mouth and runs down her throat. Color starts to return to her face, and the markings on her skin begin to glow a bright crimson instead of the usual red-orange. "I could not save mother or father, and yet, the two people I could save, I did nothing. It is because of me that Taritie could not follow us. It is my fault that Ryonis is dead."

Lyora tugs on Ashanna, but the moment she tugs, Ashanna's body dissolves like ash, floating away and disappearing into the sky.

"This child is capable of teleporting with thought. Fascinating." Lyora looks around and tries to see where the sparkling crimson dust is flying, but she cannot track it all. She does not know where Ashanna disappeared until a shrill sound pierces the dark, and a crimson glow starts rising from the deep parts of the wood. The scream also alerts Salie, who knows precisely whose scream it was. Salie starts running and stops at the sight of Lyora, pausing for a moment but overcoming and yelling, "Ashanna!"

Lyora turns away from the glow of the forest and turns to Salie. Lyora runs at her, and Salie raises her hand, still holding the polished wooden pillar, and ignites her hand. Salie holds it out in front of her. "Do not come near me, beast, or I will burn you."

Lyora starts giggling. "I have lived for a hundred of your lifetimes and seen the darkest reaches of the galaxy. Nightmares beyond what you could imagine. You could never make me feel fear."

Salie sends forth a stream of flame aimed at Lyora. Lyora dodges and grabs onto Salie with one hand and, with the other, goes for a swift strike to Salie's neck.

Lyora expects to see Salie close her eyes and sleep, but she is surprised when she does not. She looks over at her hand and notices it is gone. Her arm is deep inside a crimson portal and never made contact with Salie. Lyora tries to pull out her arm from the portal, but burning crimson red ropes appear and wrap around her. They struggle to pull her inside. Lyora stands her ground without much effort, but the ropes are only a distraction. She does not see the second portal behind Salie or the dozens of balls of pure energy hovering above and finding their place to rain down onto Lyora.

Ropes wrap around Salie and start to drag her into the second portal. Lyora keeps her grip on Salie, refusing to let go. It becomes a struggle between two different portals. The ropes that surround Lyora start to dig into her flesh, and she howls in pain. Her grip on Salie falters as she is taken from her grasp. Both portals now disappear, returning Lyora's arm intact. Lyora howls in anger up to the sky, and that is when she notices the trap above her. She freezes for a fraction of a second before she begins running. The balls of energy chase after her and explode the moment they impact. Lyora screams as her fur and flesh sear, filling the night with the complement of unhinged laughter from Ashanna.

The crimson glow grows brighter and nearer to the burned and injured Lyora. Despite how that attack would kill the average person, Lyora is still moving. She is wounded but capable of standing on two feet. This sight makes Ashanna grind her teeth.

"That was meant to kill you," Ashanna growls from somewhere in the forest. She suddenly appears from the brush to approach the downed Lyora.

Lyora smiles, and her eyes light up at the sight of Ashanna. Lyora's mouth opens, and drool flies from it as she apologizes to the sky. "I am sorry, my lady; I do not think I will be able to take her alive."

Ashanna crosses her arms. "If you know you cannot win, stop now, and perhaps I will spare you."

Salie has been watching the fight from a distance. It is horrifying. Two unhinged monsters are about to begin a second round, and only Salie can see the numerous creatures from all over the undercity watching this fight as if it is entertainment for them. Salie wants to say something, but one look into Ashanna's possessed eyes tells her that her words would not reach her.

Lyora lets out a chuckle. "Spare me? Clearly, you are not as focused as you should be. You will be lucky to survive me. After all…" Lyora starts stretching and cracks her knuckles and neck, "I am going to tear you limb from limb."

Lyora, with a startling burst of speed, darts at Ashanna, and if it was not for the distance between the two, Lyora would have reached her. Ashanna leaps and hovers above Lyora. Ashanna sends forth numerous ropes made of energy from her fingertips, and when Lyora dodges them, the ropes transform into string-like blades that start to chase after and follow Lyora, who runs along the ground. Lyora jumps onto a large rock and, from the rock, jumps up at Ashanna. She manages to grab Ashanna and throws her to the ground. Ashanna groans from the impact and flips over to face the sky. She sees Lyora above her and raises her hands, creating a ball of energy, blasting Lyora far away. Ashanna rises, grunting from the pain of the impact. She hovers up from the ground again and watches Lyora. Lyora, undeterred, prepares to attack her again.

Ashanna grins wickedly. "You can take a lot of abuse. Let me see how well you can take this." She channels all of the energy within her body. With one hand, she focuses a majority of that energy, and with her other hand, she creates crimson red ropes that trail down to the ground.

Lyora's charge toward Ashanna is suddenly halted by the massive ball of energy that hurls her to the ground. When the ball explodes, she screams in agony. Ropes attach to the burning Lyora and fling her against the trees, rocks, and everything else as Ashanna uses her like a ragdoll against all of their surroundings. Lyora tries to get the ropes off of her body to no avail, and she only stops flying around when she hits a rock and latches onto it.

Lyora's body aches, but her head hurts most of all. At some point, she received an impact to her skull that is making her head ring like a bell. She uses her free hand to check her wound while hanging onto the rock with her other hand. She pulls it back and notices blood covering it. She turns around toward Ashanna. The small girl is not much better despite receiving only a single strike from Lyora. The demand Ashanna is putting herself under is exhausting her body.

Lyora breaks the ropes attached to her and hurls herself at Ashanna. She grabs her with an iron grip and then pulls her to the ground before flinging her against the flat side of a large rock face. Ashanna gasps and tries to use more energy, but her body becomes limp. She convulses as she fights to move, but with her energy depleted, she can move no more.

Lyora walks up to the fallen Ashanna. Lyora grabs her head and roars in her face, holding the roar as her gaze shifts to the sky. With triumph filling Lyora with invigoration, she drops the body of Ashanna, places her foot against Ashanna's head, and prepares to crush her skull. Something stops her and she turns to face the forest.

Numerous pairs of eyes have patiently waited in the forest until now. With the fight clearly now finished, they begin to advance. Lyora looks upon the creatures from various distant planets across the galaxy. She flings Ashanna's limp body away. The creatures charge at Lyora, and she charges at them. Chaos ensues, and a new battle begins.

Salie is ignored by the beasts for a reason unknown to her. She overcomes her anxiety and moves closer to Ashanna, grabbing her by her feet and dragging her away from the fight. She tries to figure out where she can go, and that is when she looks toward the colossal pillar that appears to be the center of the undercity.

Salie stops when she notices Lyora being flung down into the river chasm below. Salie runs to the edge to see what is happening.

She notices the large body of the intimidating insectoid hiding in the hole in the wall from before, the same creature that dragged the knight's body into the darkness. When the battle nears, the insect surprises Lyora. Her screams fill the night as the insect drags her down into its burrow. Its mighty poisoned fangs pierce her flesh. The beasts then disperse, and everything returns to normal in the undercity. Salie looks on, horrified, and starts to vomit down the side of the cliff. She hears a loud snap like something breaking from within the insect hive and does not know whether it is from the insect or the bones of Lyora. Either way, she has a confident feeling that Lyora and the beasts of the forest will not be bothering her anymore today.

CHAPTER EIGHT:
LONELINESS

Mylos leads Taritie deeper into the royal citadel. The central structure is a prominent spire, with numerous external floating bands and secondary spires held in place by artificial gravitational devices that keep everything in the air. The secondary spires are all connected by a web of gravity shoots, where pods can be shot in one direction, reverse the flow, and fired back. In all of its grandeur, the citadel now seems hollow and broken compared to Taritie's memories of long ago. Many of its alternate spires and bands have fallen. Much of the gravitational technology remains active and causes significant gravitational anomalies and disturbances. The anomalies keep everything within their field afloat as if frozen in time.

Before the war, during the time of immortality, Taritie remembers staring at his models and pictures of this place. Developed with so many technologies working together to make something so beautiful. Taritie strolls down the path and stares at the destruction and ruin of this monument. He looked to that spire for hope when his life became increasingly meaningless. His faith and trust were in the potential of his people and that one day, more could still be achieved. That is one of the reasons why he joined the project of being frozen in time, the good and healthy reason. He wanted to see what would become of his people in the future. He knew he would be working with a team of people, and none were similar to him, but he believed that he could handle the loneliness. After every day, he would go back to his room and stare for hours at the live picture of the capital, and he would focus on the citadel especially. Knowing in his heart that his people were flourishing gave him hope and strength. Now, this seems only a reminder that his people are gone.

He looks over at Mylos and watches him continue to walk, unfazed by the empty hallways, power suits still containing and preserving bones, and the countless debris-covered murals. Mylos almost seems content, and Taritie cannot tell if it is because he has been living here for some time and is numb or if he no longer feels emotions. Perhaps a worse conclusion is that he is content with what has become of the capital because he prefers it this way.

Taritie finally musters the courage to break the silence and asks, "Have you ever told yourself you were strong enough to handle something just to find later that, well... it is much harder and more painful than you thought it would be?"

Mylos gives him a puzzled look, then smirks. "Yes, it is a concept called 'Life.' " He turns back around with a small chuckle.

They continue to walk through the long hallways, with Mylos talking about meaningless drivel and acting as a tour guide of the citadel.

Taritie finds how he rattles on irritating, but he makes no move to stop him. While he drones on endlessly, it allows Taritie to reflect on his thoughts. It slowly leads him to the problem in his mind that desperately needs a conclusion.

Arriving at the grand spiral hall of the citadel, Mylos hurries over to a unique white pillar in the center of a collection of thrones. The pillar has a built-in diamond stone, a beautiful blue stone with small diamonds scattered about, and large diamonds in key spots on the stone staircase lined with purple and gold carpet that leads to the thrones. Among the thrones some are larger, indicating importance.

Mylos flies up the staircase and over to the grandest chair facing the door, plops himself down, and makes overdramatic gestures with his hands outreached. He announces, "Enter, my pawn, and kneel before your king!"

Taritie rolls his eyes and examines the rest of the spiral hall. The hall seems endless because that is how it is designed.

Starting from what seems like an average hall with a balcony up above, it transitions and divides into four separate paths that defy gravity using gravitational devices. The hall continues to spiral and has numerous pillars that connect to each of the four paths. The hall is designed so that anyone on any of the four halls may look upon the thrones in the center of the hall where the royalty and council would sit, and depending on where you were in the hall, you were able to see different members of the royal house and high council. The two most significant chairs were saved for the High Royal and Grand Counselor.

Taritie moves past the thrones and to the other side of the hall. The spiral hall slowly converges back to how it started. On this side of the hall, giant statues of heroes, scientists, philosophers, inventors, and other great Shappalans line the converging paths and end with a large mural depicting the Feylin founder and creation of the first immortal. The first immortal was the Feylin's assistant, a Shappalan who later became the first Shappalan High Royal of the nation of Shappala.

Taritie moves through the grand doors and notices that past the hall is a large atrium that he remembers from exploring the citadel. This atrium leads to the command center, one of the capital's three main mechanisms. The others are the heart and the control towers.

The doors open again, and Mylos enters. His eyes show

just a split second of cold calculation and curiousness. He measures up Taritie and wonders if he could kill him. The answer comes quickly and is a resounding yes. Under normal circumstances, Mylos would have no trouble making short work of Taritie. Mylos looks down upon Taritie and sees him as inferior. To Mylos, it does not matter if Taritie had any training before he was frozen because the cold truth, in Mylos' perspective, is that he is younger and has never tasted the fire trial that was the grand war.

Taritie starts examining the relics in the atrium. "I am guessing these are war relics. I do not remember seeing any of these in my picture of the capital."

Mylos reaches his hand out over the display cases of weapons. "That is correct. The High Royal spent most of his time in the command center, so he brought his relics here. These weapons you see here are of immense significance."

Taritie moves over to a knife with a description that reads, "Death's Resurgence: The weapon that took the first life in eight thousand years."

Reaching out, Taritie touches the knife's blade and feels it. After feeling the cold steel and the special runes and wires inside, Taritie asks, "I was frozen before the war happened; will you tell me what started it?"

"True conflict would not erupt for a while after what

many would say started the war. Academics argue it happened when the cure for immortality was invented, but that is not what started the war. The catalyst that led into the war was when it was unknowingly administered into all of those innocent souls frozen in time."

Taritie moves to a hefty tome detailing the backdrop for the first battle amongst the stars. "So, you are telling me that my people believe I am responsible."

"What?" Mylos exclaims with surprise clearly written on his face. However, as Taritie stares at him, he sees the emptiness in his eyes. He has mastered his facial muscles well, but there is still something he lacks. "That is certainly a jump in logic."

"It is true, is it not?" Taritie looks over at Mylos and studies his face. Taritie notices a subtle upward twist of the corner of his lip for a fraction of a second and then it disappears.

"I cannot lie. You picked up on it quicker than I thought you would." Mylos picks up a sword and swings it around. "I guess I should not have mentioned it was administered to those frozen in time."

"Are you seriously saddened that you could not play with me longer? I knew the moment you saw me that you recognized me. I spent two hundred years with Feylin and Selestia scientists who had lived longer than our lives put together. We could not equate to the years they lived, and I learned there are some tells and gestures that, even after eons, are hard to hide. In fact, some become easier to tell. The only thing I did not know was why you knew me and what purpose you have for me."

"Yes, you are sharper than I believed you to be." Mylos moves near the command center door and, in a dramatic fashion, spins and bows. "You have bested me. I have known from the start that you were Taritie, the one who started the war. The one whom the elderly curse, adults abhor, and children laugh at."

"Tell me, was it you? Are you the one who invented the cure for immortality? My role in the Selstia project was to adapt the subjects' bodies before entering sleep. If anyone was to be blamed for those frozen to become mortal, it would be me. Are you the one who put it in my hands and did not let me know?" Taritie grabs the knife and grips it until his fingers turn white.

"What will you do? Fight me? How useless would that be? I know you cannot kill me, and I certainly can kill you." Mylos puts back the sword and feels the weapons rack before grabbing a beautiful spear.

Taritie continues to stare at Mylos, unblinking. Eventually, Taritie places the knife back on its pedestal. "I will not fight you. Now tell me the truth, who are you?"

"I am Mylos, the great general that led armies against the Feylin and Selestia. The one who oversaw the burning of every homeworld of all the races, including my own. I am the one who fired the mortality bomb that made everyone mortal. I froze myself in time to see what would become of those who would awake," Mylos pronounces triumphantly. He swings around the spear several times before piercing the ground with it and declaring, "I am the one who ended the war, and you are the one who began it. Two sides of the same coin."

"At least I now know something about you. Now answer my previous question." Taritie walks back and forth, waiting for his answer.

Mylos walks toward Taritie. "No, I did not do it. Are you happy now?" He examines Taritie's face. "I see fire in your eyes. You do not believe me. I suppose that comes with the trade, but I promise you I am not the one who did it. At the time you were given the cure to immortality, I was not even in any position of power. I was a hopeless philosopher and not even a famous one."

"Why hide this from me, then?"

"I did not know you could handle the truth yet."

"Do you know who tricked me into administering it? Did they somehow know what my true intentions on that project were?"

"Yes."

"Tell me who."

Mylos turns around and starts to walk away from Taritie.

With a flick of his wrist, he lazily replies, "No."

"Why will you not tell me?"

"What importance does it have? The people who lied to you are all dead and that information serves no purpose. What would empty names and titles serve you other than that you may dwell on them and curse them in your late hours? I could even make up names for you to hate, and it would have the same effect."

Taritie goes over to the wall next to a corpse and slumps down next to it. He knows that knowing who wronged him would not help him, but the sting of the betrayal is fresh. While he had believed he was helping his people in his research, the reality is he has had a blindfold over his eyes. Taritie has memories spanning hundreds of years, and yet the memory of who handed him something on his final day before being frozen blanks in his mind.

Mylos lets out a long sigh and shakes his head before saying in a gentle tone, "Rest, Taritie, I will give you some time to absorb."

Mylos leaves the room. In his absence, time seems to slow to a crawl, but the thoughts do not cease. Breaking from the racing whirlwind of his mind, Taritie notices the armor of the corpse next to him. The power armor is rich in design, and the beautiful black and gold trim signals him as a royal. Taritie notices the seal on him, which marks that he is not just any royal but a high royal. His hand is gripping a journal. Taritie reaches down, grabs the journal, and starts flipping through the pages.

The book details the final days of the war and includes, near the end, the siege on the capital. He reads the laments of many other people who wrote in the book, likely family members and friends, who each give their accounts of the events. At the end, there is a special entry, caked in blood and written hastily as if the person writing it was dying.

"Long have been the days of late. After burning the homeworlds of both Felyin and Selestia, they refused to die in peace. Instead, they have brought their war to our home, and it seems desperation breeds strength." Taritie flips the page and scans until he finds another interesting passage. "They have breached the first district and continue to bomb the others. They have already poisoned our atmosphere just as we have poisoned all of theirs. The mortality bomb has been fired, and all of us shall die eventually. The common folk and even some among the royals believe that I and a select few have somehow remained immortal, and while I entertain their thoughts, I cry in my room at night. For there is no way to reverse the effects of mortality, and none more than myself desire this to be untrue."

Taritie briefly lowers the book and looks toward the door leading to the command center. Flipping a few more pages, he reads: "General Mylos has just proposed a cease-fire and meeting. The Feylin and Selestia ships have all been shot down, and their forces outnumber ours in our own home. We are all dying, and I imagine I have less than a day." Taritie sees how the words continue and flips some more until he is on the last page: "I may be delirious because of pain and fear of death, but I am enjoying my life again. I managed something that I thought I could never do in my entire life. I have always been so selfish, yet today, I have sacrificed my life. My last act was my greatest victory in this war. That I should lay down my life for that of my daughter. The time-frozen capsule, hastily constructed, is our last hope as it will carry on two lives, a man and a woman, who will restart the Shappalan race. I have chosen my daughter and that of the general who fought so hard for me. His acute intellect and ruthlessness will be perfect for whatever trials they awake to. I pray they may find a new start and peace in the world to come." After reading it, Taritie snaps the book closed, pulls out a knife, and tosses it in the air as he mulls over a new problem and another lie that he has been told.

"Why did I have to be right about Mylos? Why could he not have been a child frozen in time instead? Why could the Shappalan race not restart with someone innocent of sin and blameless in my sight?" Taritie pauses for a moment and looks at himself. "Why did I not choose to send someone else in my place? I could have sent my sister or even had a child of my own." Taritie laughs momentarily, remembering how much it costs to have a child. Remembering that even if he worked for a thousand years, it would not come close to the cost of paying to be allowed to have children. He thinks to himself that he could have just had a child anyway and been executed like his own parents were. After all, a child would be worth the cost of his life.

"Who am I kidding? What good is having a child if I cannot be there to live next to them? Abandoning him like I was? Condemning him to live in the gutters of an already overpopulated society?" Taritie looks over at the dagger covered in lies that claim it took the first life in eight thousand years. Taritie starts to roar in a peal of mad laughter, remembering his parents, "We are all hypocrites, are we not? Look at us. A race of selfish, lying, and betraying bastards! All of us. Why is it that the monsters are the ones who always seem to survive and continue to propagate like flies?" Taritie tosses the knife upward again and willingly lets the knife impale his hand. After he pulls out the blade and the wound heals, he says, "I know what must be done. I gave my word to someone important whose life has lasted but a breath of mine. Now it is time to uphold it."

CHAPTER NINE: BETRAYAL

"Where are you, Mylos? Why are you making me have to look for you, you soulless monster? You have been holed up in that command room for days, and I know you can see me. Why are you not coming to meet me?" Hannia bellows while pulling along Ryonis, whose hands are wrapped in rope. Ryonis reluctantly follows while continuously focusing on regaining his strength and energy.

Hannia kicks open the doors to the memoriam of the heroes of Shappala. The large hall is one of immense grandeur, similar to everything in the Citadel. The building is needlessly long and tall. It is overly dramatic in all of its features. Statues of all the heroes stand in the hall, and the size of the statues determines their reverence by the royal family. If the long stretch filled with statues is not enough, their weapons, epitaphs, scenes of their famous moments, and loved ones all float above and around their statues. Hannia expects to find

Mylos here, considering how much time Mylos spent in this hall before the freezing. She would sometimes join him in staring at and reading the exploits of the heroes in hopes that she would one day be on those walls. However, that future has faded away now.

Hannia tries to push the negative thoughts out of her mind and lifts her head while walking beside the heroes. Raising her head, she finds something she did not expect, which turns her face pale and raises a long-seeded fury in her core.

Inside the walls of the Memoriam, a virtual screen appears at the furthest end of the hall. Above the large doors that leave the hall is a holographic display that casts an image of a figure sitting outside the command room. Ryonis, who does not know what is going on and does not have eyes that can see far ahead, is confused by Hannia's sudden change in demeanor. He thinks she is frozen up until the moment all her muscles start tightening and visibly expanding. Her armor, which seemed unnatural, now begins to show the reason why. The joints of the armor glow with a visible golden energy, and Hannia's body starts growing taller and more muscular. Ryonis, seeing her going manic, takes the opportunity to create a knife of ice with his mouth and starts cutting his bonds.

Hannia, with fire in her eyes, sees her quarry in front of her and, to her surprise, finds herself freezing. Her great sword is gripped in her hands now, her body enhanced and ready to fight, and yet her mind is rushing with what she should do. The figure in front of her was always like the shadow under the bed and never seemed truly real. When Mylos told her that he may exist and that she should find him, the idea of genuinely finding him seemed distant. Yet now he sits in front of her, twirling a knife and looking completely lost in thought. Hanna's blood boils in anger. Does he not know the harm he caused and the hurt he created?

She starts to walk toward the door, and that walk transitions into a run. Despite the anger inside her, she cannot help but smile. Madness bubbles up inside of her like a sickness that no amount of time can fix. She feels her body screaming and celebrating. She has been feeling so empty and hurting ever since she awoke. The ache in her chest that nothing could ever solve, yet now she has the perfect opportunity to take out her frustrations on someone, making her scream with glee and joy.

Taritie rises from where he sits, conceals the knife, and opens the door to the command center. Mylos is sitting down, relaxing while watching a screen that seems to be centered on a strange woman running. Mylos switches the camera's output to another area of the Citadel and turns to face him. "Taritie, it is good to see you joining me. I figured you would brood out in the hall forever."

Taritie approaches Mylos, sitting down in a chair and scooting within arm's reach. Looking into Mylos' silver, lifeless eyes, he says, "Mylos, I have a few questions, and I want you to answer me honestly."

Mylos yawns and stretches out his body, though Taritie can tell he was attempting to subtly put his body in a more defensive position. After yawning and rubbing his eyes, he says, "Hit me with whatever you have on your mind."

"Are we the only Shappalans awake that you know of?"

Mylos studies his face for a moment and, with a fake smile, places his hand on Taritie's shoulder. "Did I not tell you when I saw you that you were the first I had seen? Did my warmth not feel genuine to you?" It is clear to Taritie that he is testing him as much as the opposite is taking place. While Taritie wants to understand and find his conviction to do what must be done, Mylos is also mulling over what to do. These questions and responses are a game between two wisened liars to see who is the better con.

Taritie takes a moment to figure out how to reply. "No, your warmth felt genuine when I first met you, and I was just overwhelmed to see another of my kind." Taritie's words seem to make Mylos let down his guard.

Taritie looks over his shoulder at the screen, and Mylos turns to see what he is looking at. Taritie takes this moment to leap from his chair and thrust his knife into Mylos' chest and, acting on Mylos' surprise, grabs Mylos' knife right as Mylos does, and the two fight over it until it is flung across the room.

Taritie places his arm against Mylos' throat and presses down. "Stop moving, or the blade will be dislodged, and you will bleed to death. I know you are mortal, Mylos."

Mylos wheezes out, "Why would you do this, Taritie? We are all that is left of our race."

Taritie chuckles bitterly. "I know that there is another Shappalan and that you have known about her since you awoke. A fact that you hid from me. When you saw me, there may have been a little joy to see another Shappalan, but I want to know the real reason why finding me was so lucky for you."

Mylos clutches at Taritie's arm, trying to relieve some of the pressure on his throat. "Do you mean sweet and impressionable Hannia? I wonder how you found out about her? But, that is no consequence now."

Taritie presses down further. "Answer me, what is it you hope to accomplish?"

Mylos tries to chuckle. "If you had asked nicely, I may

have even told you. Now you will just have to figure it out for yourself. There is one thing I can tell you, however," Mylos licks his lips and leans near Taritie's ear. "It is going to be rather painful for you."

Mylos spits in Taritie's eyes and begins to laugh. With him blinded for just a moment, Mylos grabs the knife and kicks Taritie off of him. Taritie falls back and wipes the spit off of his eyes to see Mylos, of his own volition, pull out the knife and throw it to the ground. Mylos lifts his shirt to reveal the wound where Taritie stabbed him close up and mend itself.

"That is impossible. The cure for mortality should still be in your body."

"It is, and soon it will be inside of you as well."

"I do not understand."

"You are the scientist; why do you not just figure it out?" Taritie jumps for Mylos' dagger on the ground as Mylos flies forward and shapeshifts his feet into large talons that grab Taritie's shoulder and crush his bones. Taritie had reached for the knife, but it fell to the ground with a thunk as Mylos carried him into the antiquary and through a side door that led to a large, ruined chamber that may have once been an amphitheater or meeting room of some kind. The ceiling of the room is open, and light spills into it.

Taritie shapeshifts his hand into claws and slices up at

Mylos, creating an opening in his grip. Taritie slides off and hits the ground, breaking his legs. Taritie's legs heal almost instantly. It takes longer for his shoulders and the rest of him to repair, but he is eventually fully healed. Mylos takes position across from Taritie in this large amphitheater.

Mylos swiftly plants his spear firmly into the ground of the vast amphitheater. He turns to Taritie and asks, "Do you recognize this place, Taritie? It is a setting that holds many memories for our people."

"No, it looks like a place you would have a play."

"It is similar. This is a room where the greatest minds of Shappala would entertain ignorant fools with grandiose displays of marveling theological and philosophical debates. A room where I spent my youth, staring up at great names such as Myrius, Filusti, and Salconthidensius."

Mylos continues to prattle on while Taritie ignores him, trying to understand how he could have healed so quickly. If the cure for mortality is inside of him, there must be another way that he is healing. Taritie did not see him use any spray, salve, or other healing tincture. He may have a biological injection to heal him, or perhaps a biotic enhancement of some sort.

Mylos finishes whatever it was he was rambling about and waits for Taritie to reply, only receiving a blank stare. He sighs. "I see my breath is wasted on you. You were just a slum child who received his education through cheap sources. Still, I was once a philosopher, and if you want answers or for me to change my ways, I will give you this chance. I am willing to listen and debate one last time as a philosopher in this place, the forum of the capital, a place holy to me."

Taritie has already given up hope of changing him and understands this is just a game, but still, there may still be answers he can get from this. "You told me that if I asked you, you would tell me what you hoped to accomplish by lying to me. What purpose do I serve in your plans?"

Mylos gives him a fiendish smile. "Weak first strike, Taritie. This is a battle of wits, and yours are too shallow." Mylos puts his finger on the butt of his spear and spins around it. "You ask for what purpose you serve. I have sought an answer to that question, and it is worthy of this forum. Tell me, what is the purpose of creation?"

"If I humor you, will you answer my question?"

"Perhaps."

Taritie sighs and tries to remember his philosophy classes. "The Egosum Gathering of Shappala would argue that purpose comes from understanding the mysteries of the universe and coming to a knowledge of our creator."

Mylos nods his head and runs his hands through his hair. "You did not strike me as a religious man, Taritie." Mylos takes a moment to gather his thoughts. "I have argued with many from the Gathering over this question and believe that answer a hollow and pitiful reply."

"I spit your words back at you. You did strike me as a religious man, Mylos."

"Truthfully, it is hard for philosophers just as much as scientists to believe in anything because we are so linear and foolish in our thinking. We cannot trust anything we do not fully understand."

Taritie furrows his brow. "In that line of thinking, creation has no purpose because you cannot visibly lay a standard for something as intangible as purpose."

Mylos scoffs at him. "Incorrect. Intangible ideas require different proofs but can be explained and even proved, just as gravity cannot be seen but is understood by our people. If you were more knowledgeable, I would quote many great thoughts, but it would be mere noise to you." Mylos turns away. His dramatic display makes Taritie grind his teeth. "Back to the question at hand, though. The Egosum Gatherings argument is flawed because it would imply our very reason for creation is to make others aware of the creator and knowledge of him. This is flawed for many reasons. Namely, if the Gathering succeeds in this purpose, they no longer have any more purpose. What egregious thinking!"

Taritie rubs his eyes. "I am lost."

"Imagine if your goal is reading and collecting books by a certain author. What happens when you collect all of them?"

"I do not know. I guess you find a new book and enjoy it?"

"Precisely! You have answered all of what I have come to understand in such a simplistic and beautiful way!" Mylos pulls from his pocket a journal. "The Gathering's goal of making everyone aware of a creator is like this book. This book can be completed, and then it no longer serves a purpose other than to be looked back on with fondness. Once our purpose ends, there is no longer any reason for creation. The obvious conclusion is there must become a new purpose."

Taritie, keeping up with Mylos' train of thought, nods his head cautiously. "Okay?"

"Let me put it another way: our lives are meant to end so a new story can occur. A new drama that can be enjoyed. With immortality, our lives become like a play that drags on longer than it should. The only pleasure comes when the boring scenes come to an end."

"You are talking about why you created the mortality bomb."

"There was no passion anymore. The mundane routine and monotony became unbearable and needed to end. Perhaps I was even curious to see if I could eliminate every story but mine, and then I could watch to see if a new story would begin."

"You are mad. I saw through you when we first met, but in my selfishness, I said nothing."

"You have not lived long enough to understand. Emotion leaves you; the world becomes so dull that meaning ceases to exist. All lives become useless. Can you even call my actions murder when those are the lives I am ending?"

"You want deep thought? Let me show you what a child born from nothing is capable of. I am not knowledgeable in history or your great philosophy, but I have experience. Life is valuable and should be treasured, not something you have the right to end based on your skewed values. You are no better than the scientist who murdered my parents."

"You say this, but your actions contradict you. I have seen the file written about your life. You devoted your entire life to killing a Feylin doctor. He killed your parents, and so you lied and conned your way to get close to his side. Then, by some unknown method, you found a way to kill him without the cure for immortality. Then you ran away to wherever you hid a secret time freeze capsule, and with your own injection, you put yourself to sleep and remained immortal while all those you froze became mortal."

"That is different. He was like you, a monster."

"You just said that life is valuable. Are you saying that

certain lives are not? Because that is precisely what I am arguing. We are one and the same, two sides of the same coin. You believe those without your view of ethics or morals should die, and I believe those without my view of passion should die. Who here is right, and who is wrong?"

Taritie groans, fatigued from the complex discourse. "You are twisted. I do not have words to express how you are wrong, only that you are."

"I wish we could debate more. If you were given time, perhaps we could come to an understanding. Oh, how I long to be understood. Alas, our time here is at an end." Mylos grabs his spear and takes flight away from Taritie. He throws some kind of dart at Taritie, and he falls limply to the ground. The venom is strong and seems to paralyze him swiftly. His body burns the venom away, but the paralytic effects linger in his system.

The door to the ruined forum opens, and a large woman storms in. She looks up at Mylos and asks, "Where is he?"

"Where is who?" Mylos playfully replies, smiling. The look on Mylos' face is one of superiority, and it seems he is enjoying every moment of his betrayal. Taritie watches Mylos radiate with confidence and joy, and it makes him feel sick.

"Do not screw with me, freak; you should have told me the moment you ran into him," the woman berates Mylos. He does not seem at all intimidated by her and rolls his eyes before gesturing down at the crippled mass that is Taritie.

Mylos hovers over him. "Give him a moment to heal if you want a fair fight, or just beat the immortality out of him if that is what you desire. Either way, when you are done having fun and have exhausted his ability to quickly repair himself, drag him to the heart of the city." Mylos does not give Taritie another look before flapping his wings away from him.

Hannia runs down the steps of the theater. "Where are you going?"

"I am going back to the command room. There are a few things I must prepare for."

Hannia stomps her foot defiantly. "You ask a lot of me, Mylos. I have killed more immortals than you have despite how long you have lived, so you have no right to order me."

"I am the only one that has access to the cure, so if you want to kill him, you will do what I tell you." Mylos begins to fly away, but briefly stops in front of the door to the ruined chamber, turning back to smirk at her. "Unless you want to turn him into a pet, that is up to you."

Hannia gets flustered and hurls a stone at Mylos, who dodges by quickly closing the doors and leaving Hannia alone with Taritie. With Mylos gone, Hannia steadily walks down to the crippled Taritie and plants her blade into the ground before sitting down on the stone and staring at Taritie. "The moment you are done healing, we will fight, and I will break your body. You will answer my questions while you heal again, and then I will repeat the cycle until I am bored. Then I will drag your screaming body to Mylos, and he will perform whatever experiments he wants. I assure you that your death will be agonizing."

Taritie groans as feeling begins to return to his limbs in the form of pins and needles. "Well, if my death is assured, do you mind at least telling me your name? You are the daughter of the head of the Royal family. Does that make you Hannia?"

Hannia stands up and walks over to Taritie. She raises her foot, and Taritie raises his hands to protest. In a flash, Hannia stomps his skull into the ground. "If you are strong enough to ask questions, then you are strong enough to fight. Next time, you will let me ask the questions."

It takes about a minute for Taritie to reassemble his face, and after doing so, he comments, "I think I remember your temper being noted by one of my colleagues who had met you. He was a Feylin named…"

Hannia interrupts Taritie by taking her sword and decapitating his head before kicking it into the wall. This time, it takes a few minutes for his head to slowly move back to his body and reattach.

Hannia scowls. "I did not ask. You will answer only my

questions."

When Taritie's head finally reassembles, he says, "If you keep destroying my head, how can I?" Hannia slices his torso in half, and Taritie bites his lip, trying to maintain himself despite the pain. "On second thought, please destroy my head. It is less painful."

"Stop talking so that you may fully heal, and we may have a proper fight. I take no pleasure in beating a helpless whelp." Hannia glares daggers at Taritie, who smiles at her in return, causing her to cringe.

"Good to know I am not the only one who is uncomfortable here." Taritie begins to laugh half-hartedly. Hannia waits for Taritie's torso to reattach before she ignites the energy in her blade and shoves it into Taritie's chest, pouring energy into him that melts his midsection and bringing out the first authentic screams of agony from Taritie. Within a few moments, Taritie is unconscious.

Ryonis, after escaping his binds and watching Hannia storm away, looks up to see the source of her change. A strange transparent screen made of light reveals Taritie. He now understands why she ran away, but the fear in his chest tells him he needs to leave. After seeing how Hannia transformed before him, he has no desire to step into a fight between creatures beyond understanding with his current strength. He does not second guess his luck and starts to make a break the same way he came in. Running as fast as he can, he makes his way down the long halls and through the numerous and seemingly needless chambers.

While descending a large staircase, Ryonis notices a blue string attached to his body and a second one passing by his face. He reaches for it, and the ethereal string passes by and around his fingers. The string is created by tiny droplets of light gathered together. Ryonis tries to mess up the string and even freeze it to no avail.

A voice calls out to Ryonis, surprising him. "Ryonis, you are alive!"

Looking up, Ryonis sees Ashanna and Salie moving to meet him. His eyes go wide at seeing them. He first notices a small lizard with wings perched on Salie's shoulder. The little, tiny dragon with beautiful red scales and blue eyes is the one creating the blue string that extends from the breath of the dragon. Ryonis cannot help but give a broad smile and rushes down the stairs to greet both of them with a hug. When he hugs

Ashanna, she pulls back, and Ryonis sees that her body is badly beaten and bruised. He reaches out his hands and feels the large swollen knot on her face. With gentleness, he cups her chin before pulling back his hand. "I guess I am not the only one who has had my share of adventure."

Ashanna smiles at him just before she raises her hand and smacks him. With an agitated yelp, Ryonis pulls away in shock.

Ashanna glares at him. "Because of this crazy demon named Lyora, I thought you were dead. Do you know how worried you made us when you disappeared? Thankfully, Salie called her pet, showing us you were alive. On top of that, we find you perfectly okay and running about here while we have been desperately searching for you!" she finishes her rant with a shout.

Ryonis gets up and tries to explain. "I did not mean to worry—"

Ashanna grabs him by his collar and shakes him. "I do not want your excuses; who are these people that took you, and why did they let you go?"

"To be honest, I have no idea who they are." Ryonis points up the staircase. "Past those doors and a couple of chambers further down, I escaped the woman who took me. She is... she is a Shappalan." Ryonis hesitates to say. After all, they are like myths. In his mind, Taritie is, in a way, an exception because he has known Taritie for a long time. The idea of Taritie being any warmonger or monster simply seems impossible to Ryonis.

"Okay, why take you alive? The lady who attacked us also mentioned something about capturing us. Does that mean we have some importance?"

"That is because of me, probably. She is searching for Taritie; we are important because we know him. However, I do not think we can play that card anymore."

Salie looks confused and presses, "What do you mean?"

"I saw Taritie, and it is actually because of him that I could escape." Ryonis finishes this sentence, and Ashanna starts tearing up. She raises her hand and goes in for a slap, but Ryonis grabs her hand. Salie then slaps Ryonis, causing Ryonis to pull away from both of them. Ashanna then steps forward and slaps him across the face harder than ever.

Ashanna roars, "Taritie risked his life to save me, and he has saved you plenty of times before, and instead of helping him, you are running away like a coward!?" After this outburst, Ashanna trembles and falls to her knees, coughing. The injuries she gained from her previous battle still hurt her, and she cannot go into another fight of the same caliber.

"What was I supposed to do? While she was carrying and then dragging me, I had little time to regain my energy, and there was no way I could have fought against her. After all, her servant did this to you, and if I went up against her, she would have killed me like swatting away a fly." Ryonis protests and Ashanna cannot even speak through tears and wheezing from pain.

Salie helps Ashanna up and starts to carry her up the stairs. Salie looks back and tells Ryonis, "You fought beside Taritie as a comrade in arms. Would he have ever left you behind?"

Ryonis clenches his fist until it turns white and bites down on his lip until it starts bleeding. Ryonis was following his instincts. There was no use in fighting a battle when all he would do was die. Even worse, he could hold Taritie back, and he could never forgive himself if he died because of him. It would be better for everyone if he just ran away.

Despite his excuses, Ryonis knows what he must do, and he cannot remain still any longer. He turns around and, catching up, he reaches out his arm and lends Ashanna his shoulder, carrying her up the stairs.

CHAPTER TEN: PRINCESS

Taritie opens his heavy eyes, the pain still clinging to his mangled body and his thoughts a dense fog. With slightly blurred vision, he realizes that he is being dragged. With all the intention he can muster, he narrows his gaze to what his eyes can perceive: a ceiling of rich white and gold in hexagonal patterns. Looking to the side are the walls containing murals and rich lanterns, though few remain intact, and even fewer are lit. He continues to struggle, but his body does not seem to respond. Looking down at his body, he sees his chest has not fully healed. A large indent still remains in him with seared and burned flesh.

Taritie tries to move and see where he is being taken, but before he can get his bearings, he is thrown against a wall. The impact causes him to groan, and more of his blood seeps out of his body to the ground. That little impact knocked out any strength left in his body. Even as an immortal, he cannot do much without sustenance.

While leaning against the wall, Taritie takes note of his surroundings. The room is centered around a raised circle in the middle used for sparring and testing weapons. The rest of the room consists of numerous circular chambers and rooms where many weapons and armor float suspended in the air.

Taritie tries to speak, but nothing comes out of his throat. He realizes that both his lungs must have been melted with the attack, and he will have to wait for them to heal. He expects that now would be the perfect opportunity if Hannia wanted to tire out his regeneration to the point that she could drag him to Mylos without incident.

Hannia squats down next to Taritie and reveals some ointment. She begins applying it to Taritie's chest, and the injury is completely gone within moments. However, because she used the salve instead of letting Taritie's regenerative abilities heal it, there is now a large scar where the wound once was.

Hannia covers the salve and stows it back on her person before grabbing a ration from a pocket beneath her surcoat, which she throws on Taritie's lap. She explains, "I know my pity is wasted on scum like you. However, it is beneath me to fight you in such a one-sided manner. I have dragged you to the armory. Here, you may rearm as you need to and tell me when you are ready to fight a true duel." Hannia grabs a chair and sits down across from Taritie. Her eyes are fixed on him, and she waits patiently and silently.

Taritie scarfs down the ration and soon afterward rises and looks about the room. He says, "I truly expected you to take me straight to Mylos. After melting my midsection, there was no way for my body to heal itself for another hour without some food. You could have easily killed me if you wanted to."

Hannia crosses her arms and leans back in the chair. "I may have acted savagely at first, but I promise you that I have values and beliefs that are more important. I will not merely relieve my anger on you like a beast does and kill you without, at the very least, allowing you to defend yourself." She stands and walks over to some of the armor, examining them.

After several moments, Taritie has yet to determine what weapon or armor will give him some edge in this fight. He tries to focus while his mind dwells on Hannia's words.

He picks up a large spear on the rack and feels its weight. "Mylos believes that age is the ultimate determiner of who will win in a fight. While I disagree, you likely have a key advantage in experience and training. What is the point in letting me fight if the outcome is already determined?" Taritie, resting the spear, grabs a longsword with a beautiful design and engraving. The blade's sheath reads in old Shappalan, "Immortality reveals the need for discipline and duty."

"Mylos is wrong about many things. He is sick in his mind. That trait is something that many of the admirals and royals of the end days shared." Hannia starts stripping an armor stand of its equipment and throwing it on the ground before Taritie. "Put that on."

Taritie looks down at the silver royal guard armor beneath his feet. "If you disagree with Mylos, why do you put up with him? Why do you not go out alone and live your own life?" He feels unworthy as he lifts up the helm, gazing at its gleaming visor as if staring at a person within.

He starts to strip down to nothing but his undergarments to fit inside the armor. The armor has built-in temperature control capable of withstanding the heat of most energy weapons for a limited time, a sturdy impact layer, the ability to expand and adapt to the wearer's size, and the capability of expanding around any new body parts or additions the user may create using shapeshifting.

"I put up with him because we are the last of our kind."

"There has to be more than that."

"There really is not, so stop prying." She punctuates her sentence by kicking one of the greaves on the floor.

Before touching the armor, Taritie pulls his chosen sword out of its sheath. The blade is a remarkable work of craftsmanship with beautiful ornate silver metal and intricate designs throughout the blade and handle. The length of the blade is covered in writings and slots where the energy will pour from inside and form the rest of the blade. Compared to his previous longsword, the energy blade is superior in all regards.

While practicing a few swings with the sword and giving his body time to rapidly digest the food, he is now at a height that he could give a good fight. However, when looking at Hannia, he understands that being equally equipped will not be enough. "When I went into the Selestia program for time freezing, I understood I would be alone and leaving my own people behind, but I did it because I believed the cause was worth it. Little did I know how unprepared I truly was. How alone and dark every night became to the point I dreaded the time I was not at work."

"Is that why you betrayed your people? You felt alone?" In her narrowed gaze, the guilty verdict is already given, but there is a tiredness and curiosity that perhaps can be exploited with the right push.

Taritie sheaths the blade and leans it against the wall. He equips the armor at his feet. "It was a relief to go to sleep, and it was a mighty surprise when I awoke on Shappala. However, the excitement of being home soured after a few days. Without its people, this world could never feel like home; it felt empty and made my longings worse." Taritie pauses for a moment, now having the armor on his body. He examines himself and stares up at the decorations and decadent luxuries, which, in his eyes, do not belong in an armory.

Taritie glances at Hannia. "When I learned that there may be survivors, funny enough, there was no relief. Only new anxiety sprouted and grew in my mind. I believed I would have to fight them and perhaps kill them because they would be monsters created by the war. However, just as when I entered the time freeze program, that was another more difficult promise than I had first believed. When I saw Mylos, it was like a cool wind on a sunny day, like water in the desert that is my soul."

"You still have not answered my question. Unless you want me to decapitate you... again, I suggest you answer. What made you betray your people?" Hannia growls. He can see the limit of her tolerance is fast approaching, and none of his emotional appeals seem to humanize him in her eyes.

However, she does groan as she scratches her head as if she could scratch away some intrusive thought. "You were on the program; you should have known how many scientists were checking and rechecking the capsules. Why would you commit such an obvious sabotage?"

Taritie pulls from his discarded satchel the singed journal of the High Royal. He tosses it to Hannia. She reads the front cover and the name of its author, her father. "Page seventy-four includes the date and time the cure for immortality was created by a scientist named Frigurd. You should note that during that time, I was already enlisted and a part of the time freeze project, and all communications would have been cut off as a part of my agreement with Selestia. I had no means of knowing the cure had been created."

She turns to the aforementioned page, briefly scanning it before shutting the journal again and scowling at him. "This solves nothing. You had help from the outside, and more people were involved than I had previously thought."

Taritie stretches with the armor on and fetches his blade. With an uncomfortable sigh, knowing this will be hard for her to understand or believe, he says, "I read through your father's journal. I read through all of it. If you read ahead twenty pages later, he describes how the decision was suggested to the high council and royal family of starting a war with the other great nations."

"I do not believe you; this has to be all lies." She flips through the pages again, but instead of reading, she throws the book away and stands on her feet. Her eyes are wavering, and her hands are shaking. Her form shrinks to a size only a little taller than himself, and it is clear that her powers are reacting to her emotions and not responding as they should.

"Selestia wanted to declare war, but Feylin offered

Shappala an alternative in the form of a hearing and counsel. The Feylin emperor believed the Immortality Cure administration was an act of terrorism and wanted it to be treated as such. Shappala willingly chose not to attend and started the last great war."

She sneers at him. "Your words are a venom. I should have dragged you to Mylos instead of entertaining this nonsense." She places her helm on her head, and despite her change in form, she still seems capable of wielding the massive sword and igniting it with energy. She steps up on the raised circular platform and gives a gesture that invites him to do the same.

He sighs. "I am sorry. I hope that if you choose to kill me, you will at the least discover the truth. These ruins are still alive, and all their secrets are in your hands." He lowers the visor on his helm and examines his blade until he finds the groove, where he presses down and ignites the energy in his sword. It streams like water and forms with an intense radiating heat. He steps up to the circular sparring platform in the middle of the room, planting his feet in a solid stance and readying his blade so that it points at Hannia.

In an instant, the duel starts with full force and the swiftness of the wind itself. Hannia is the first to make a move. She darts forward and closes the distance between herself and Taritie. She tries to shapeshift into her potent form but she still seems incapable. Instead, she compromises with a level of change of about the same strength as Taritie's. She slams her foot into the ground like an anchor for her near-unstoppable momentum. Her strike has enough force that the wind whistles with her blade.

Despite the impressive show, without her superior enhancements, it all seems slow to Taritie. He parries the thrust and uses the opportunity to counter with a downward slash that hits her helm but does not slice through. His blade instead bounces off, and she slams her blade into him. He briefly imagines his body cleaving in two, but the armor somehow holds up. An orange glow is left on the armor, and his insides are evidently ruptured, but nothing will stop him from fighting, with immortality playing its part. The part that causes Taritie to worry is how his body flies back after the strike. It becomes a desperate effort to maintain his place on the platform.

With the momentum carrying him out of the ring, he thrusts his sword into the ground, managing to stay inside. With a sigh of relief, he rises from the ground and reclaims his stance. A surge of confidence pours into him, and he is ecstatic to survive crossing blades with her.

In her fury and anger, she charges, further pressing her offense, leaving herself open for attack. Hoping that her strikes will not give him room to strike, she unleashes a series of consecutive blows from which Taritie dances. Her overly large sword does give her an advantage in keeping him at a distance.

Her onslaught begins to slow, and Taritie chooses to take advantage of this. He blocks an attack and sidesteps past her blade and into close-range. He raises his own blade to prevent her from swinging the sword back into him.

Hannia releases a hand from her blade, causing the point of her blade to hit the ground, and goes in for a punch. With Taritie having more momentum and seeing the attack coming, he takes the chance to strike her with his pummel toward her face.

The attack does little but annoy her. She responds by completely letting go of her blade, grabbing a knife from her side, igniting it, and thrusting it through the lower part of Taritie's armor and into his abdomen. He reels back from the attack and tries to recover from the burning pain. The only consolation is that because of all the pain he has already endured, this pain feels numbed and not as intense as it would have been otherwise.

With Taritie reeling back, Hannia can withdraw the blade with her right arm and aim for his face. Relying solely on reflex, he slashes his blade up at her and manages to make an impact with that same arm. The blade connects with her armpit and does not bounce back. Her blade is almost touching his throat, and in her fury, she screams out and tries to force her arm to go further. The pressure presses his sword deeper into her arm. She falls forward before understanding what is happening, and her right arm does not come with her.

Taritie pushes her off and takes a step back. She quickly gets up and gets in her stance but realizes something is off. Hannia, in confusion, stares at where her arm is meant to be for a moment before the realization hits. With this realization comes the pain, and she lets out an intense scream, falling to one knee. Despite this injury, she refuses to give up. Her pride not letting her admit defeat, she leans back, grabs her large blade, and attacks Taritie. Her attack is a precise strike despite her shaking body and non-dominant hand, showcasing her countless years of training.

Taritie admires her will to fight, but it will not change her fate. It is a simple matter for him to kick her backward and pin down her remaining arm. He slams his pummel into her hand until she lets go of her blade. To his surprise, he feels her knee impact his abdomen and she manages to force him off of her. She struggles to get up and makes a move for her sword but second-guesses herself and instead turns and goes for the knife. Taritie, recovering from her kick, goes after her and prepares to strike her from behind.

Hannia is directly in front of him, and he has the full

capability to kill her, but he hesitates. That hesitation is all it takes for Hannia to grab the knife, turn around, and thrust it up into his chest.

With his sword, he only has to hold it to her leg while she tries to thrust the dagger deeper. Within moments, the metal is bubbling, and Hannia falls to the ground, screaming in agony. Taritie continues until her leg detaches from the rest of her body. She struggles and fights to get her footing, but he does not feel the will or desire inside of him to finish her. He raises his blade above her while she looks up to him with fear and anger.

She screams, "I refuse to die here!" She grabs another blade from her side and throws it at him. The knife bounces off, leaving only an orange glowing scratch. She pauses, catching her breath. She throws off her helm and grits her teeth.

Realizing defeat, she lays back, letting tears stream down her humiliated face. She closes her eyes and waits to be finished off, but the next thing she feels is something thud off of her armor.

Hannia opens her eyes to see that Taritie has thrown the salve from the table. He brings over her detached arm and leg, saying, "Even with that salve, you may want to sit and rest for a while. I suggest you take the time to read your father's journal."

Hannia, through her tears, says, "Do not leave yet."

"There are children here that I need to protect. None of

them are safe until Mylos dies and the capital is returned to how it should be."

"You were not able to kill him, were you?"

"He is not immortal, I do not know how he is doing it, but I am certain I can find a way to kill him."

"That is how fools think."

"Do you know a way for me to kill him?"

"No, but I may have an idea of where his power comes from. I fought him after I awoke and could not kill him." She grabs the salve and her detached limb. She puts her limb onto the cauterized wound and drips the salve around the corners of both wounds. The salve brings life back to both sides and begins to connect the unattached limb, undoing the burn and reviving the once-dead cells. "I believed the rumors that perhaps he found a way to become immortal again, but that cannot be true. His body is aging still, and his healing has no cooldown, unlike your body."

"How does this help me?"

Hannia does the same to her leg and lays down momentarily, breathing in relief. She informs him, "During the final days of the siege and after he awoke, he lived in the heart of the capital. He worked there day and night with many scientists and brilliant minds. He said his work was on defending the capital against intruders, but his goal may have been something else. I am certain the answer you are seeking is down there."

CHAPTER ELEVEN: CONTROL

Ryonis had at first believed the blue string the dragon breathes to be miraculous. In a way, it is, but it happens to be a major inconvenience as well. The dragon does not directly show someone a path to the person but instead tracks all of their movements. While Ryonis would have been lost without it, they have been to room after room in this vast spire, and now it is taking the group somewhere else.

Ryonis groans as his impatience grows to new heights. "Salie, is there no way for the beast to take us on a more direct path?"

"You have to trust it; it will bring us to Taritie." Salie takes a moment to rest, causing the whole group to come to a halt. She reaches up to scratch the chin of the beast.

Ashanna seems to perk up and suddenly jumps in front of everyone defensively. "Someone is coming."

Ryonis pulls out his book and steps up beside her, ready to

attack and, if need be, jump in front of harm's way for her.

Salie pulls out her obelisk, holding it out in front of her. "There is not just someone in front of us. There is someone behind us as well."

Ryonis and Ashanna turn around, and indecision takes Ryonis. He continues to guard the front, and Ashanna moves to the back. All eyes go back and forth until, from the direction Ashanna guards, a bestial and bloody hand appears and grabs the wall. It turns the corner, and the figure is almost unrecognizable. Missing an arm, numerous large stretches of skin, an eye, and its armor in tatters, the beast Lyora slowly advances toward them.

She lets out a roar that causes spit and blood to fly toward them, splattering across the floor and their clothes. The warm, wet feeling is enough to pull them out of their shocked stupor and they abscond in a moment.

Over the sound of their swift footsteps and the continued roars, Ryonis asks, "Ashanna, did you do that to Lyora?"

"Some of the burns were from me, but the rest was from monsters in the undercity."

"Monsters did that? How the hell is she still alive?"

Salie says, "I saw her get dragged down into the den of a huge insect. I have no clue how she survived."

Lyora's roars grow louder, and she catches up to Salie at

the back of the group. She grabs onto her and is about to bite into her when Ryonis pulls his knife and shoves it into her jaw. Lyora throws Salie at Ryonis and prepares to tear them limb from limb when a loud voice can be heard from a room at the end of the hall, ordering, "Lyora! That will be enough. Return to me."

Lyora drips blood from many parts of her body, especially where she had just been stabbed. She pulls the knife out from her jaw and drops it on the ground. Her eyes glaze over, and she limps like a wounded dog over to her master.

Limping past Salie, Lyora glares daggers at Ashanna before passing by completely and smiling deliriously at Hannia through the doorway. The group hesitantly follow the blood trail and peek into the armory room.

Hannia, in bad shape of her own, is slumped against a wall with blood smears all the way to the place she is sitting now. Her voice is soft. "Lyora, my friend, what have they done to you?"

Lyora grabs some of the salve, rubs it on her tongue, and waits a moment before speaking, "You should know those children could never hurt me this much."

"What caused all of this, then?" Hannia stands up on her two legs and wobbles momentarily but steadies herself.

"I have never seen anything like it. The undercity came alive and attacked me."

"The undercity does not just come alive." Hannia leads

Lyora through a door on the other end of the armory. Through the use of a lever, the back wall opens, and from it, a new room is revealed. The room contains a miniature medical station, although the children and Salie do not understand the use of nearly anything in the room.

Hannia guesses, "Mylos saw an opportunity to get rid of you without me knowing, and he activated the undercity from the command center."

"You believe Mylos has betrayed us?" Lyora lays down on a table, and the machine above her activates and repairs her. It starts by injecting a sedative and applying a mist over her that causes her skin and even hair to return. From where her missing arm is, metal is implanted, and a mechanical arm is assembled and replaces the void.

"I believe he has done what he has always done: serving his own interests." Hannia continues to mess with a terminal and oversees the operation.

"My lady, in my condition, I will not be of much use to you. I am afraid death's door is before me; I have lost too much blood, and poison courses in my veins."

"I expect you to rest and get some sleep. You have done enough." Hannia walks over to Lyora and attaches two IVs, one with blood and another with a clear liquid solution that seems to make Lyora relax. Hannia goes back over to the terminal and continues to press buttons. A cybernetic eye descends from the ceiling, and mechanical arms implant into Lyora. The eye has long, thin wires that seem almost alive, and they squirm and move to fasten themselves inside Lyora's skull. The sight is enough to cause Ashanna to gag. When the procedure is completed and the machine stops moving, Lyora is fast asleep.

Hannia turns and faces Salie. "You are all friends of Taritie correct? The ones he spoke of, those he must protect."

Salie steps forward. "I am Salie. To my right is Ryonis, and to my left is Ashanna."

Ryonis says, "You were hunting him. He was the one you called prey, right? What use is there in answering honestly if that will make us your enemy?"

Hannia rubs her face and seems exhausted but answers, "It has been a complex and interesting day. I have had more mental bombshells unloaded on me today than I have in the thousand-year period I would have called my youth."

"Well, does that mean you will not kill us?" Salie asks.

Ashanna almost looks offended. "Why do you think she can kill us? I went toe-to-toe with that Lyora beast while you sat back and watched. With all of us together, I think we could survive her."

Hannia scoffs and pats Ashanna's head as she walks past her. "I can tell who the simpler of the three of you is."

Ashanna turns cherry red, and the energy lines in her body glow. "I am in no way simple; you take that back."

Ryonis sees what is happening and keeps his mouth shut, but he snickers. He knows what Hannia can turn into and the fear it inserts into him, but seeing her now, he does not have that fear. She is wounded and seems almost pacified. Despite this change and her wound, he would not go as far as to believe they could survive a fight against her.

Salie interrupts the banter, trying to get back onto a useful topic. "Back there, you mentioned that someone named Mylos activated the undercity. I remember Taritie mentioning that everything in the capital is controlled by a command center. Is that where we should go if we hope to run into Taritie?"

Hannia thinks it through for a moment and turns to Salie. "Believe me, you want to be nowhere near Taritie or Mylos."

Ryonis chooses to step forward. "I need to redeem myself; I will not leave Taritie behind as I did before."

Hannia answers the boy's courage: "Mylos is in the command center. By now, he has seen that Taritie is loose again and will activate the Citadel defenses. Within fifteen minutes, the entire citadel will be swarming with machines, and not even Taritie will be able to reach Mylos. You will be torn limb from limb if you go after him."

Ryonis clenches his fist. "There has to be something we

can do."

Hannia walks toward the door. "Yes, there is something we can do, but it is a long shot. The command center is not the only means of influencing the city."

Salie steps forward and, with steel in her voice, says, "Whatever we can do to help Taritie, we will do. He has saved all of us, and we plan to return the favor."

Hannia stops for a moment and laughs half-heartily. Looking at the three young warriors, like children, ready to lay down their lives. None of them comprehend just how much of a monster Mylos is. Well, one of them perhaps does. Hannia looks specifically at Ryonis, who has seen her transform and had felt genuine fear, now stands ready to face someone stronger than herself. She needs to find out if this says something about them or Taritie. The way they revere and will do anything for him astounds her to the point she feels stupid for believing that Taritie could have ever been the villain that her people made him out to be.

Ashanna, who seems to dislike Hannia for no apparent reason, asks, "What is so funny?"

"You are," Hannia tells her before gesturing to all of them. "You all are." She takes a moment to admire them before gesturing for them to follow her. With no better ideas, the group eventually submits and starts to trail behind her as she leads them down more of the clustered halls of the citadel. She takes them to a shaft, and when she steps inside it, a flow of gravity launches her up. Salie is the first to gladly jump inside the ancient tech, her dragon still on her shoulder. Ryonis is second, and Ashanna, not trusting Hannia, is the last to reluctantly to step inside.

Salie gasps in excitement. "This is like that gravity river we found that launched us near to the spire, Ashanna. I am so glad we found that, or else we may have never caught up with Ryonis." Her voice manages to carry down to those beneath her.

Ashanna, being the last and the one who trusts the lift the least, watches with fear as air blows against her. She clenches her teeth as she continues to fly faster up the chute. The tube becomes brighter, and the walls disappear until nothing keeps her from falling. The light of the sun shines down from above and illuminates the gorgeous ruined capital below. The lift continues upward, and when Ashanna looks up, there is nothing but blue sky. She starts to breathe rapidly and panic rises within her until the lift slows down. Then, she is gently tossed over to a balcony connecting to an extraordinary, beautiful tower with a roof resembling a bulb covered in small statues.

Unlike Ashanna, who is still trying to slow down her heart from the shock, Salie is happy to have her heart racing. Her heart beats faster and faster as she marvels at the beauty and architecture of the Shappalan people. She looks out over the edge and realizes this tower is being suspended by nothing, which makes her mouth fall open in wonder. She starts letting out incomprehensible sounds of glee and excitement. She follows the edges of the broken railing and fixates on all of the strange images and designs on the floor and walls. She comes to the door of the tower and sees words she recognizes above it. She looks up at the words above the door, pulls out her journal, and tries translating the old language. "Control tower master?"

Hannia leans over Salie and glances at her scribbled writings. "Close, but that word you translated as 'tower' is actually 'citadel,' and the proper way to order the words would be, 'citadel master control.'"

Salie starts hastily writing things down and drawing the words inside her journal. Ashanna and Ryonis walk past her and enter the control tower. The room is circular, with a sizeable hologram that is shifting and filled with occasional static. Parts of the lights dangle down, and the room is covered in remains of machines and the hollowed-out armor and power suits of whoever must have been defending this room when it was taken.

Hannia says, "When Shappala was attacked, they had to take each of the control towers before they could poison our atmosphere. We developed counters to the devices they used, and they had to disable them before they could render our planet a wasteland as we did theirs. This was the last control tower they took, and the moment it was captured, the end was written."

"How will this place help Taritie? It looks like nothing here works." Ryonis asks, lifting a group of wires and staring at the numerous colors.

"What I need still works and that is all that matters," Hannia assures Ryonis. She moves a hollow, dusty armor suit out of a chair and sits down. The moment she places her hand on the console, it comes alive with light.

Ashanna looks at all of the strange machines and terminals she does not understand. "You said Mylos is in the command center. What is the difference between the command center and control tower?"

The light of the terminal connects with Hannia's head, and it is clear to most that Hannia is seeing things the others are unable to. Scenes and numbers whiz past inside the reflection of Hannia's eyes. She answers, "The control tower focuses on the environment of the capital, electricity, water, atmosphere, doors, and a host of other things. The command center focuses on the command of all machines, biochip-controlled creatures, turrets, energy cannons, everything along those lines. The command center also has functions dealing with the heart of the capital, but I do not understand how those work."

Ashanna starts to get bored of things she cannot comprehend and stops trying to keep up. Half of the words out of Hannia's mouth were gibberish to her. Yet Salie, who had just entered the room, was writing it all down as if it was some new religion. Ryonis, on the other hand, stares blankly into space, and it is clear he is in his own little world. All these words are likely rattling past his brain.

Ashanna, having had enough of the futuristic jargon, asks, "What can we do to help Taritie? You brought us up here. Now tell us what we are going to do."

"Patience, Ashanna, I will explain everything in time."

"Your version of explaining is throwing words I do not understand. In that way, I see why you stopped fighting Taritie and got along."

Hannia looks back and asks, "Ryonis is your name, right?"

Ryonis wakes up from staring at space and whips his attention at Hannia. "Yes."

"Are you still capable of fighting?"

"Yes, I can still fight."

Hannia looks over at Ashanna. "I am just going to take for granted Loudmouth can fight." Ignoring the indignant glare, she turns her gaze to Salie. "You seem the least combat-oriented and the smartest out of this lot. Are you capable of putting up a defense, or should I leave you here?"

Salie meets her gaze steadily. "I refuse to be left behind. Wherever you are going to help Taritie, I want to be there."

Hannia spends a second longer on the terminal before stepping back and away. A light in the center of the room turns on, emanating from the floor, and a loud sound like wind activates. Hannia stares at the light and takes a deep breath.

Salie watches with curious eyes. "What did you do, and what does that light do?"

"I have just activated the teleporter and shut off power at the command center. I cannot stop whatever commands he may have already sent out, but I can stop him from doing anything more. I plan to breach the heart of the capital, take direct control over the city, and find a means of killing Mylos."

Ashanna huffs and puffs before complaining, "In words that normal people can understand, please."

"That light will take us down to the center of the city. There, we kill the bad man."

Ashanna bunches her fists. "I am not five years old!"

"You could have fooled me with the way you act."

"You are insufferable. I do not know why Taritie let you live."

"I do not know how Taritie can put up with you."

Ryonis, having enough of the arguing, jumps into the light. "I hope this does not kill me." In a moment, he appears on the other side. Ryonis pauses for a moment and takes a second for his eyes to adjust. Having come out the other side, he checks himself over to make sure he is all in one piece and that he has truly been teleported to a completely separate place. The technology of the ancient nations is beyond spectacular despite him not understanding any of it.

When he heard they were going to the heart of the capital, he expected to find himself deep within the ground, but this was not the case. He stands on a balcony of a building that looks to be built by giants. From the terrace overlooking the city, he is even able to see past multiple walls all the way to the entrance from which they first came. The structure he stands on is a strange stone building covered in green overgrowth. A structure with a church-like shape and astounding detail and numerous larger-than-life statues depicting scenes of things his mind cannot understand or comprehend. The statues show men talking in some scenes, others show a man whose ear has been cut off, and other statues show scenes of death and, even more, numerous creatures with wings. While beautiful, Ryonis wonders how the building he stands on is somehow the city's heart.

He turns and sees a door and stained windows inside. Through those windows, Ryonis sees that inside this church built for giants is what looks to be a large altar. At the very back of the altar, there seems to be some sort of lift with a mural depicting a heart and vines reaching out and lifted by angels. Ryonis is no expert, but that would be what he would guess is the heart of this city—the place that all of them came here to find.

Salie is the next through the gate. She says, "I had enough of those two bickering as well. I wonder if that is what I usually sound like."

Ryonis turns toward her, shocked to hear Salie sounding so casual. He expected her to be mesmerized, but she seems almost too quiet and not interested. Salie licks her lips and looks around, and her eyes start to go wide. She passes out and hits the ground with a thud just as Ashanna and Hannia come through, still arguing.

Ryonis watches Ashanna, hoping that seeing where they have been transported would quiet her down, but the moment Ashanna notices her surroundings she shrugs it off and continues arguing with Hannia. Ryonis sighs and chooses to head down the steps of the balcony, toward the main sanctuary of the church where, hopefully, the lift will take them to the heart.

Hannia turns away from Ashanna and looks out over the balcony. She notices a startling lack of movement around the church. The center of the capital is meant to be under constant security from numerous machine guards, yet those guards are nowhere to be seen. Either Mylos wanted them to go inside the heart, or those guards were moved to another secret place he deemed more important. This is a dangerous sign, considering the guards that guard the heart of the capital are a foe that Hannia has still not determined if she could handle at the peak of her strength, and right now, she is nowhere near that peak.

CHAPTER TWELVE: CURE

Taritie arrives at the command center to find the doors locked. He examines the door and knocks on it, examining the sound to see if the blast doors have also been activated. Feeling confident, he ignites his longsword and begins to press it on the door. The locked door soon begins to melt and give way to the blade's tip. After a couple of minutes, a new door is made. Stepping inside, Taritie enters the command center and finds a dark, abandoned room.

Taritie takes a moment to look around the room before noticing that a secret door has been opened on one of the walls. Going through the passage, it leads further up the citadel. Taritie believed the command center was at the top of the citadel, only to be proved wrong when the light started shining through, the walls disappeared, and the passage turned into a series of open golden stairs that climbed to the citadel's peak.

To be on top of the citadel is akin to being on top of

the world itself. Large golden pillars, with silky drapes flapping in the wind, create a pavilion with a dainty chest-high railing surrounding the octagonal-shaped platform. In the center are four desks and multiple tables where studies and small experiments have been taking place.

Mylos stands in the middle of this pavilion next to the tables. With a half-mad smile, he throws binders of papers which are caught by the wind and taken into the sky. He searches until he finds a large metal cylinder, and he pauses and lets out a breath, looking up and meeting Taritie's eyes.

His smile is that same familiar warm glow that he has seen before. Undoubtedly seeing Taritie as an audience, he begins, "There is nothing more worthless than a philosopher when everyone is immortal. All problems cease to have meaning. Living itself becomes pointless and mundane." Mylos pricks his finger and places it on a metal cylinder. The cylinder begins to open up, and a vial of liquid is revealed inside of it. "That is why when the cure for immortality became public knowledge, I leaped at the chance to be a part of its distribution. I wanted to be a part of bringing back purpose to this misguided world."

"That is the cure? That small vial is what began the war and cut short countless lives?" Taritie instinctively recoils from it.

"Short? Would you call the Feylin, who lived for tens of thousands of years a short-lived race?" Mylos shakes his head and laughs. "No, we were living too long and needed to restart."

"Mylos, what is it you are doing? What are you planning?"

Mylos lets out an annoyed sigh and gestures to Taritie as if he should figure it out for himself.

Taritie glares at him, taking a couple of intimidating steps forward. "This is the last chance I will give you, Mylos. Explain your plan to me, or I will have no choice but to fight you."

"Because it went so well for you last time." Mylos reaches down behind his desk and raises his spear.

"When I stabbed you in the command room, it was a mercy."

Mylos chuckles spitefully. "A mercy? What do you believe you are saving me from? Who do you believe you are? A worthless scientist born in the gutter with no name or value."

"It was a relief when I believed you were mortal. It meant I did not have to revive something I thought I learned for only one man." Taritie recalls those green flames that reside in his soul. The flames still burn with hatred to this day.

"Are you sure you do not have royal blood? You almost sound like them."

"Will you not answer my question?"

Mylos sighs once again, sounding even more irritated. "I have told you everything you need to understand. Why are you unable to figure it out? Should it not be clear as glass?"

Taritie finishes stepping over to Mylos and looks down at the research before him as if it were all some puzzle. "If I had to guess, you want to play god and have created something that will allow you to do so."

Mylos laughs. "Yes and no; your verbage is quite ironic because playing god is what our people did during our supposed golden age. Removing the most key element, the part of us that gives us purpose. Mortality is not a curse but a gift. Because we suffer with this knowledge, we have to make each second count. We had lost that. That is why the mortality bomb was the only answer."

"You believe you have helped the universe by taking so many lives?"

Mylo looks at him with a twisted smile. Taritie looks upon him, and a chill travels up his spine. The man in front of him seems sick and beyond saving. It reminds him of when he was a young college student visiting the execution prisons. Seeing the many people who were too unstable to be kept with the general public. At the point where it was more unethical to allow them to live. Taritie had to meet and even talk with some of these prisoners before being executed via transference. (Transference, one of three highly secret methods of killing an immortal before the cure, is a month-long process of transferring immortality from one person to another. This process was often used when parents would have a child they did not pay for, and the government would transfer immortality from the parent to the child.)

"Yes, I believe that with all my heart." Mylos declares brazenly. His eyes taunt Taritie to try doing something about it. Mylos reaches behind him and presses a button, and his desks lower down into the floor. The free-flowing silk cloths near the columns are tightened and become walls around the pavilion. Mylos in a very showy fashion, places the cylinder with the cure for immortality in the center of the pavilion.

"You once said that we could come to an understanding. You believe in your twisted logic with all your being and long to have someone to understand you. Well, I do understand you, and I say that you are more deserving of death than all those you have slaughtered combined. There is no cure for your madness." A familiar anger boils within him. Heat rises in his chest and green flames begin to bud like flowers on his body. Taritie takes a stance, but this time, it differs from his fight with Hannia. He thinks back to the knife he found in the atrium. He chuckles internally at the irony of its title: "Death's Resurgence." At a young age, he has known death in an age where the public is told no one dies.

Long before the cure for immortality and even before the more humane means of transference, the Feylin, the bringers of immortality, had an issue. Their resources could no longer keep up with their growing population. Food became scarce, prisons overpopulated, birthing laws unenforceable. Their solution came by the means of a radical in their government, a scientist studying the specifics of immortality. Immortality binds the soul to the body, and only by cutting those threads can one reverse it. This led to the creation of the soul cleave. The ability to shatter the soul and the threads that bound the soul to the body. There is the philosophical issue of the ultimate fate of the soul and the effect of cutting it, but what did it matter when the initial problem was solved? They needed people to test it on, and to that sick scientist's delight, there were countless subjects he could choose from.

At the age of eight years old, a year after his parents had been imprisoned, he and his sister were dragged behind glass to look upon his parents. Initially, they planned for transference when he and his sister reached adulthood. But that all changed when they sat him down and told him to watch. A memory that no matter how old Taritie grows, he can never forget. He watched from behind glass as his parents were brought before the Feylin scientist who had created the soul cleave. He listened to the scientist as he explained everything he was about to do. The scientist smiled as Taritie's mother and father cried and screamed in agony, consumed by green flames. Taritie watched the process unfold, the scalpel glowing with a green light as the scientist ripped into his parents and tortured them before finally ending their lives. It was a memory that determined the path of his life.

Mylos giggles to himself and plays with his spear before eventually readying himself for a fight. He steels himself just as the wind starts to blow and ruffle the silk walls. High above the world, a duel against the last two immortals was about to take place.

Mylos, even as he still holds an advantage in years, looks unsure of himself despite how he feigns confidence. "Do you want me to fight with an arm behind my back?"

"Enjoy your last moments, for the sake of those I have sworn to protect and for those beyond the grave who cry out for your end."

Ryonis leads the way through the church pews and past the large golden columns. Despite being beyond beautiful, the church makes Ryonis feel sad. There is something empty and hollow about the place, and even the ways the statues are created make them seem to lack a sense of life, with empty and hollow eyes. It is almost a talent that the architect can display this feature despite the fact that the statues are smiling and made of shining gold.

Hannia says with trepidation in her voice, "Ryonis, back away from the lift."

Ryonis stops for a moment and looks around, as if some enemy may be approaching, but nothing pops out. He looks back at her wary face. "Is there something wrong?"

Hannia nods. "Have you ever heard the expression 'The weather feels nice before the storm?'"

Ryonis looks confused. "I do not think so?"

Salie says, "No, I do not believe I have either. I have heard 'the quiet before the storm.' I feel that is a little more apt considering what I think you are trying to say."

Hannia seems to curl her lip and gives an expression like she will take note of that and remember it for future use. She comes back to the present and explains, "It is just too quiet. There should be guards here, and their absence worries me. Either they are down at the heart waiting for us, or there is a reason this place does not need guards."

Ashanna stares warily at the lift. "What are you saying? The guards are ready to ambush us the moment the lift reaches the ground?"

"The guards or something worse," Hannia adds morosely, and everyone looks at each other, confused. "I have never personally been down to the city's heart because it is off-limits, and I have heard many rumors about it." She considers her own words for a moment. "Though, considering how a majority of the rumors I have heard are false, this is probably nothing."

Salie crosses her arms. "You could have just said we should be ready for anything. Now I am terrified, and I do not even know why."

Rolling her eyes, Ashanna grabs Ryonis and steps on the lift. "We have waited long enough."

Salie meekly steps onto the lift with Hannia and looks at her with trepidation. "I wonder if I should have stayed back at the tower. Maybe you could have taught me how to use the control room."

Hannia laughs. "Yes, let me just sit you down and teach you eons of new technology in the short time we have."

The lift travels at a steady pace down, and its walls seem rather unimpressive—just regular cold and dripping stone.

Salie looks disappointed. "Is there no way you can just put the information in my head?"

"Yes, I could have done that, actually. That button was the one left to the teleporter." Hannia tells Salie, and Salie looks at her with anger brimming in her eyes.

"Are you serious? Why did you not just tell us that?" Salie feels betrayed. She could have stayed behind in the safety of the control tower.

Ashanna leans over to Salie. "She is joking." Salie looks over at Hannia and realizes she is snickering. Salie's face loses color, and her gaze lowers to the floor.

"I thought you were being serious. I felt so stupid for a moment, and now I feel stupid for believing you."

To brighten up Salie, Hannia explains, "There are devices and machines we use to implant memories from one person to another. However, the control tower did not have such a device. If we survive this, on the off chance I can find one, and the even greater off chance that it works, I will implant some memories into you."

"Are you serious? You have no idea how much I would love that." Salie's morose expression fades away as if it were never there and she begins celebrating and imagining all of the things she will soon learn. She starts aggressively jotting notes in her journal, including all of the things she wants to learn and all of the memories she wants implanted.

Ashanna and Ryonis chat with each other, and Hannia waits patiently in contemplation. A short moment later, artificial light starts to glow beneath the lift, the stone walls disappear, and a large chasm large enough to hold an entire capital district appears.

Inside the chasm is a large red and electronic fleshy core with numerous vines and tendrils reaching out to the sides. Statues, similar to the angels from above, line the sides of the chasm. These, unlike the other statues, do not hide their emptiness. Their faces look to be in agony and a deep pain that goes beyond words or understanding. They feed the vines and tendrils into pipes and cables that run throughout the city. A strong telepathic field is present here and emanates from the core as it sends commands throughout the capital.

Salie for once looks upon a creation of Shappala with not curiosity but anxiety. Her eyes see the heart of the capital and it makes her stomach begins to turn. "What is this place?"

Hannia looks back to Salie with the same expression, her hands shaking. "I have just as much knowledge as you."

The lift reaches the ground, and when they step off, the ground glows with crimson bioluminescent light. There are large puddles of red flesh mixed with technology and wires that run to the heart of the capital and separate from the massive tendrils. The ground itself has a light covering of flesh, similar to a layer of moss on stone. But unlike stepping on moss, it instills a feeling of disgust in one's body strong enough to encourage vomiting. Salie stumbles and begins to do just that, to everyone else's increasing disgust.

Hannia notices standard artificial lights from a facility and a metallic path leading to it. Walking down the path, she stands on the edge of the capital and looks over to see uncountable fleshy sacs that line the chasm beneath the heart.

Ashanna rubs Salie's back and pulls her to her feet. "Salie, pull yourself together or Hannia might leave us behind." Salie nods, wiping her mouth and taking deep breaths as she begins following the group.

Hannia leads the way into the clean and brightly lit complex, where numerous machines remain active and working. Machine creatures are also down here, but they are simple labor machines that run algorithms and ferry samples from the core. Inside the next room is a wide hallway with a glass window that looks toward the heart and extends in a circle around the entire length of the chasm. On the left side of the hall are cloning pods, and inside are Shappalans, who are being grown like animals. A tremor runs through the ground, and the pods activate in an opening sequence. Fluids begin flooding the floor as the pods release their holdings.

An intercom begins to release a warning. "Cloning pods 1-1,000 have been activated, preparing to release 1,001-2,000." A moment passes by, and an intercom announces, "Pods 1,001-2,000 have been activated, releasing 2,001-3,000." The sequence continues as the group looks at a window at a deep chasm beneath the heart, lighting up with lights as fluid pours like a waterfall down into the abyss. The sequence continues counting up. The clones begin to move and rise to their feet.

The intercom announces, "Pods 9,001-10,000 have been released, preparing to release the crimson queen." After this announcement, the intercom becomes a white noise that eventually cuts out.

A newborn, fully grown clone grabs Ashanna's arm, and she recoils back. The clones advance, and something is eerily wrong about them. The group rushes out of the hall and closes the door behind them. They are back in the experiment room, which has the path back to the lift.

Hannia rushes over to a console and desperately starts trying to understand and figure out what is happening. However, the process continues. Ryonis looks out a window and feels tremors occur more frequently. He sees the tendrils at the heart of the chasm start to move and pierce the ground above. The ceiling begins to collapse and descend. The lights in the room flicker, and power fluctuates. When the power turns on again, the door cycles from the power surge and opens and closes repeatedly until a grouping of hands reaches out and starts prying the door open. The safety sensor beeps and opens the door just enough for the clones to rush into the room.

Salie screams, Ashanna grabs a scalpel and prepares to defend herself, and Ryonis creates ice spikes and starts chucking them at the oddly aggressive clones. Hannia continues to work on the terminal and eventually announces, "I did it."

Ashanna is rushed by a clone and engages in a grappling contest with the slime-covered abomination. While grappling with the clone, Ashanna asks, "What did you do?" The machines start up a repetitive beeping sound, and after a moment, they engage the clones in combat and begin eradicating them. The sound of fighting ensues throughout the underground.

Hannia answers with a wide smile, "I mentioned before that the command center was linked to the heart of the capital. I managed to access the command center from here, ordered the machines and creatures to defend the city against hostile invasions, and registered us as friendlies and everything else as hostiles."

Ryonis inquires, "What about Taritie? If he shows up, will he be a hostile?"

"Well, if he starts getting torn to pieces, I suppose I can walk over to the console and see if I missed something, but I think he is added." Hannia rises from the terminal and helps repel the clones.

CHAPTER THIRTEEN: DUEL

A massive quake reverberates through the city. The cathedral near the center is ripped apart as crimson tendrils break through the ground and begin demolishing everything in their path. Taritie loosens his grip on his weapon, and dread fills him. He feels something strange emanating from the center of the chaos; a greater will inside the destruction that is shouting in triumph. The dread only deepens into a dark pit as he senses Ryonis and Ashanna are caught up in this horror. He turns his head, the sad and quiet expression on his face molding into a growing and regretful anger as he looks at Mylos. The flower of compassion he once had for Mylos has wilted, and the winter of his heart has come.

Mylos gazes back at him in delight. "You have been speaking of defeating me as if you are a hero to save the day, but I won the moment I activated the mortality bomb. I have enjoyed my entrée and it has made me full, but look upon my dessert."

Mylos breathes in the air and raises his arms to feel the breeze. "Can you smell it, Taritie? It is the smell of a new world, a mortal world, a purposeful world, a Shappalan world."

"I do not know what you have done, but I will not stand for it. If it threatens the lives I have sworn to protect, I will upend this very world to stop it." Taritie feels his passion flowing into him, and it takes every ounce of his being to remain calm and maintain poise and his form. Every bit of him wants to leap out in aggression and thoughtless attacks, but he has gone through too much to give in now. To give in to anger would be to give Mylos the victory. He has trained for battles such as this, and has experienced war.

Despite all of this, Taritie does not feel at a disadvantage. He still has inside him that driving force, a passion forgotten by his people, the strength that pushes him to surpass and has let him overtake everyone else.

The wind blows, nearly knocking over the vial filled with a deep black liquid. Taritie becomes entranced by the vial, with its clouds of grey swimming unnaturally inside it. The moment the vial steadies itself again, Taritie begins his approach. Taritie does not reach down for the vial but instead aims directly at his enemy. The vial is merely an unnecessary distraction, and while Mylos believes that the vial is Taritie's only hope for killing Mylos, it is quite the opposite.

Mylos looks confused as Taritie steps past the vial, and he nearly laughs at what his eyes deem foolishness. Mylos mockingly stretches out his arms to allow Taritie to get one hit in before he kills him, but something does not sit well with him. Taritie's sword arches upward, and Mylos' eyes perceive a green shimmer of flames coating the blade. Flames that get stronger the closer Taritie gets. His soul screams at him to move. Mylos' wings take him into the air, and the blade grazes his leg. He only receives a small cut, which is of no significant concern. He waits for it to mend, but the wound begins bubbling up with blood and leaking down into his clothes. A drop of blood falls to the ground and informs him of something that he is unprepared for.

Mylos, as a general, is aware of all means of execution before the cure but had never seen them, nor did they matter when the easier-to-reproduce and administer cure came to fruition. After all, the soul cleave would require anyone who wanted to wield it to master manipulation of energy that mixed the art forms of Selestia, Feylin, and Shappalan into a single art form and required decades of learning. How could that compare to a simple liquid that could be injected, coated, breathed in, applied, and used without any learning curve?

For the first time in centuries, Mylos feels his adrenaline pulsing inside his body. His blood is not just pulsing but boiling, goosebumps gather along his forearms, and his hair stands on end. He feels true fear for the first time in eons, and it makes him excited beyond what he could have previously imagined. He laughs hysterically, "I thank you and deem you worthy of my praise."

"Why are you running? Come back down here so we can finish our fight," Taritie taunts as he finally feels the tide shifting in his favor.

"Unimaginable! All the days I was a philosopher feeling empty and reaching the point of desiring death..." Mylos dramatically shivers and obsesses over the near-death experience like a child discovering his voice for the first time. "If only I had known I just needed you. You have awakened me, and now I feel restored. My soul has longed for you, my soul brother."

"Stop babbling and draw near to me. I promise I will make you feel more than what you feel now. I will rip from you your wings and fulfill the promise I gave to someone whose life is worth ten of yours," Taritie declares, and by this moment, even Mylos notices the changes in him. Taritie has embraced his rage and a hunger burns in his eyes.

Mylos' eyes go wide, and his smile wider. In a maddened stupor, he laughs and charges at Taritie. Swooping past him and grabbing the cure for immortality. Coating his blade with it, his nails, and even drinking it so it would coat his teeth, all to have the utmost chance to get a single drop of it into the blood of Taritie. This action makes clear to Taritie that Mylos' immortality likely does not come from his soul being attached to his body, and thus, the elixir has no power to separate that bond.

Mylos fears what may happen when his soul is shredded by Taritie. For if his soul is broken and nothing remains, what becomes of Mylos? That thought fills his mind and makes him quake in fear, making him feel more alive. Even worse, his soul may reform and reattach to the monster to which he attached his soul. The creature that is giving him his immortality.

Taritie watches Mylos shapeshift his body. His hands become the claws of a beast with silver fur, his legs turn into that of a bird, and a silver mane of silver feathers and fur begins growing. With a battle cry, Mylos swoops once again at Taritie, aiming his spear at him. Mylos spreads his wings and hovers in front of Taritie, rapidly thrusting in his direction and forcing him back.

Taritie feels the brush of the silk wall behind him and the air from the thrust of Mylos' spear, which is only a breath away from his neck. He acts quickly, lowering his body and striking upwards. Mylos' spear goes past and over his shoulder. He roars as he reinforces his strike. His sword erupts in green flames, and his blade enters Mylos' side and slides across his body. Mylos clinches his teeth and draws back his spear. The spear on the way back catches onto Taritie's shoulder and rips his shoulder open. Although made of the best quality, the armor is nothing compared to Mylos' unique spear. Neither of the wounds begins to heal, and blood drips onto the ground.

Taritie enhances his legs and arms. His arms start to shift and become more muscular and bestial in shape. Taritie launches forward and, trying to maintain some momentum, goes on the offensive. With a fast-paced set of slashes, Mylos is pushed back. Taritie manages to get closer and, with a burst of strength, slashes at Mylos. When the attack is blocked, Mylos is sent flying back into the silk wall. Taritie takes the opportunity to jump and slash at Mylos once again. The blade hits his spear, but Taritie changes the angle, and it manages to worm past his spear and pierces his shoulder. Mylos is in an awkward position but takes the handle of his spear and jabs Taritie in his stomach. Taritie stands strong and continues to thrust his blade into his shoulder and lodges it deep before Mylos pushes him back.

Mylos is at a disadvantage now, and he knows it. How he maintains that wide, toothy smile despite his shaking hands and glazed eyes is beyond Taritie. Either way, soon, this battle will come to a close.

Striking through the silk wall, Mylos flees into the sky and starts to encircle the pavilion. Taritie is caught off-guard by this change and tries to keep track of him, but he has trouble doing so. Mylos flies below and above the pavilion and seems to be going faster than the wind itself. The only thing that alerts Taritie of an attack is Mylos' deranged laughing. He turns around as Mylos pierces through the silk wall. Aiming his spear directly at him. Taritie sidesteps and slashes at Mylos, causing him to fall to the ground. Mylos recovers with a quick roll to his feet and charges again. Taritie slashes at Mylos but he deftly dodges and pierces Taritie's left side. Taritie raises his blade above Mylos and plunges it into his chest but the man refuses to stop moving, only letting out a blood-filled chuckle. Mylos jumps back, pulling out the blade from his chest, causing blood to spill onto the ground. His body shapeshifts to close the wound, not healing him but delaying his death. Mylos uses the last of his strength to push Taritie back with a tackle, breaking through the silk wall. Taritie feels his feet come out from under him and he reaches out, grabbing hold of Mylos. Taritie, with great effort, grabs a knife from his side. He does not hesitate as he plunges the small weapon into Mylos. His eyes turn glossy, and he finally stops smiling as tears run down his face.

Mylos' final utterance is a quiet one. "I do not want to die. I am not ready." Taritie's face is one of disgust as Mylos' body becomes limp in Taritie's arms and they are both thrown over the side of the tower.

Their descent is suddenly slowed by a gravity anomaly

that surrounds the spire. Using this time, Taritie takes his knife and cuts through the wings on Mylos' back, absorbing them into his body. If the cure for immortality was not already in his system, it certainly is after absorbing pieces of Mylos. Wings grow on Taritie's back, and he kicks Mylos' body off of him. Taritie takes flight as they leave the gravity anomaly. He watches from above as green flames from Mylos' wounds begin to grow and consume his soul and body. They spread like an infection that encompasses Mylos' entire figure. The moment his body makes impact with the ground, it is nothing but a puff of ash that leaves a shadow on the ground. Taritie grips the wound on his chest and flies off toward the church.

Even with help from the machines, the clones continue to pour out and overwhelm the group. A bright light can be seen outside the laboratory as Ashanna ignites a blast of energy, burning through and killing numerous clones. Ice follows up, pushes back, and seals the open hallway.

Salie uses what little Selestia power she has. She uses wind to push back the clones into the hallway. Hannia hits the button to shut the door and activate the blast doors, sealing the clones inside.

Ashanna feels the toll of exhaustion and groans, knowing that her energy from the fight with Lyora was by no means recovered. Another attack like that, and she may lose consciousness. Her vision is shaky, and she has a headache ringing through her skull. She carefully walks over to Ryonis. "This is crazy. We have to get out of here."

Hannia nods in agreement, which would shock everyone if they were not preoccupied. "This is beyond us. I have already activated the machines to attack and eradicate the clones, but some will undoubtedly escape regardless. The only thing I can do is activate a lockdown from here and at least keep the clones inside the city where they can do no harm."

The sounds of explosions and roaring can be heard, and bright lights start to appear. Salie runs over to the window and looks out. Everyone watches her begin to panic. "I should have just sat in the safe, cozy, non-monster-filled control tower." Ryonis runs over to look down through the window, and his eyes widen. Salie steps away from the window and starts to run out of the laboratory, screaming, "This is nuts!"

Ryonis, in a calmer but still panicked voice, says, "We need to go now." Ryonis grabs Ashanna, and both start running out of the laboratory. The last one in there is Hannia, who activates the capital-wide lockdown. She looks out through the window and sees the clones start to shapeshift into numerous inhuman forms and climb up the sides of the chasm. Four or five clones climb onto the window and pass by Hannia with only a glance. One of the clones chooses to stop and begins beating on the glass with a bear-like arm.

Hannia mutters, "Mylos, you freak, what have you created? This is a great deal more than just cloning." Hannia runs out of the laboratory and makes it to the lift, where everyone is waiting for her. After stepping onto the lift, it starts to rise. More of the ceiling of the chasm begins to fall, and more light streams inside as monsters climb to the surface. The heart of the city now has enough room to rise above the ground, and just before it does, it begins to open like a fleshy flower, and the outline of a person can be seen just before the stone walls of the lift block out all view.

The lift arrives back at the church, where large vines and tendrils pierce the ground and wrap around the many statues and parts of the church. From above, a familiar figure with wings descends into the church, dripping blood, and everyone seems excited to see him except Hannia. Ryonis and Ashanna rush to him and hug him. Salie stands beside him in her panicked state and greets him. "It is so great to see you. Would you be able to fly us out of here with those wings? Quickly? Please?"

Hannia notices a familiar gleam coming from the wound. "I do not think he will be flying anyone, including himself." She rushes over to him and separates Ryonis and Ashanna from him.

She forces Taritie down onto a pew and opens up his

armor. "You have the cure inside of you."

Ryonis, with worry, asks, "Is he okay? What does this mean?"

Ashanna, completely confused, asks, "Wait, cure for immortality? Are you telling me Taritie is immortal?"

Hannia looks over to Salie. "Could you get these two away from me for a moment? I need to see what I can do." Salie grabs Ashanna and Ryonis and brings them away. With them separated, Ryonis tries calming down Ashanna and explains everything he knows.

Taritie, in his weakened state, asks, "How does it look?"

Hannia grabs her salve, but the container is basically empty. Hannia scoops what tiny remnants remain and shoves it into the wound. To her dismay, the wound does not close. She detaches a small satchel from her armor and opens it up. Inside are numerous first-aid supplies.

She grabs a cloth first and presses it onto the wound. "Put pressure on that and keep it on there."

Taritie complies, but he feels he is going to die. "The moment I came into this capital, I knew I would find more of my kind. My soul told me that much, and I was right." Taritie raises his head and looks at Hannia. She ignores his words and focuses on patching him up with all the speed she can manage. "I also knew it would end like this as well. Fate has never been kind to me."

Hannia lifts Taritie's hand and starts rubbing and applying more of some other medical tincture to his wound. Afterward, she pours on a vial of something else, and the pain leaves Taritie's body as he sighs.

Still working furiously, she asks, "Were you able to kill Mylos?"

"He willingly ingested the cure for immortality, and it did nothing to him. However, I managed to break the ties that held him together, shredded his soul, and scattered it. Hopefully, that separated whatever was healing him. Moreover, I watched his body burn in green flames until the moment he was nothing but ash. If that does not kill him, then nothing will." Taritie answers her, and Hannia grips her chest.

"You and I are truly all that is left of the Shappalan race, then." Hannia lets out a deep breath and gives a somber smile.

"What of that creature Mylos awakened and all of those clones? I saw many of them while flying by, and they look fairly Shappalan." Taritie questions, and Hannia looks at him with irritation.

"I should not have to explain why clones and monsters do not count. You and I are the last ones, and if you are lucky, I may be willing to allow you to romance me... for the sake of our species." Hannia stands Taritie up and starts wrapping bandages around his belly. She applies pressure and moves Taritie's hand back on his wound when she is done. With a few last touches, she wipes the sweat off her forehead and grins while reflecting on her work.

"Who said I even wanted to try and romance you?" Taritie quips, and Hannia's face turns red. Taritie looks over to Salie and asks with a grin, "Salie, Hannia is talking like I am going to live. How would you like to help me foster the next generation of Shappalans?"

Salie yells out a little too quickly and enthusiastically, "Yes!" She pauses for a moment, clears her throat, and, calming herself down, responds, "I would be honored if you used my body as a vessel to propagate and save the Shappalan species. It would, after all, be easier to run experiments on my own children."

Taritie's mouth drops in shock at the answer and the reason behind it. Looking back to Hannia, he quickly says, "I made a mistake, I think I may reconsider."

Hannia slaps Taritie, and Salie is now lost in her own private world, monologuing about samples and journaling genes.

Taritie explains to Hannia, "I was just joking with Salie. I did not mean anything by it. I need time before thinking through something so huge as starting a family."

"Well, who said I was interested in starting a family? I said maybe, and now I do not know if anything is possible at all." Hannia storms off, and he can clearly hear her complaining about Taritie playing with her emotions. Her voice is loud enough that he thinks that she may be intending for him to hear it.

Ryonis and Ashanna approach Taritie, and he smiles wide at them. Reaching out his arms, he welcomes them with a hug. They embrace for a moment before Taritie takes a step back. "I could not be prouder of you two. Despite how traumatic everything has been, you have both proven yourselves. Ryonis, you managed to make sure no one died, and Ashanna, anyone else would have caved from the stress, but you must have fought so hard."

Ryonis, with his tired eyes, looks like he only wants to go to sleep, but he still asks, "What happens now? We are locked inside the capital with all these creatures and no way out."

Taritie looks at them both and how exhausted they are. He sees all that Ashanna has gone through and the hurt she has felt these last few days and wants to hug her for hours. But he knows that Ryonis is correct, and first, they need to get out before any relaxation can be done.

Ashanna says wearily, "What is there to return to? Nocturna will be waiting at the village, but other than them, no one else will welcome us back. Not anymore…" Ashanna looks grimly down and seems on the verge of tears, but something keeps her from doing so. She continues fighting it and remaining strong for everyone else's sake.

Ryonis puts his hand on her shoulder. "We do not know your father's fate. Try not to dwell on what might have happened."

Taritie wraps his arms around her and, with a soft touch against the back of her head, holds her. He could say anything, but she did not need his words. With him simply being there, she quietly begins to cry again, and Taritie holds her. Ryonis watches quietly.

After a few somber moments, Taritie announces, "Ashanna makes a good point. There is nothing to return to outside these walls. More than that, we may open or show the creatures inside means of escaping in our own attempts. Our only option is to make our home inside the capital, and here we can live fruitful lives guarding the outside from the dangers that still lurk inside this place."

Salie gazes at him in slight horror. "What about the monsters? Will you be able to protect us from them?"

Ryonis adds, "What about food and water? We do not even know the layout of this place."

Salie begins pacing back and forth. "Evil mutant clones,

strange red awakened monster, red vines taking over the place, corpses, bizarre animals, dangerous hidden secrets... all in all, this place is a horrible place to live."

Hannia interrupts with a cough and steps forward. "I have lived here for months, and if you want a place of safety, I know that the agricultural district is mostly isolated from the other districts and will have food and water."

Ryonis looks at her with that tired concern he has had for a while. "How do we know that we will be safe? Something that we do not understand and have no means of fighting against has just awakened."

Taritie reaches his hand toward his shoulder. "We will survive. More than that, we will thrive here."

Salie pulls out her journal and begins jotting things down, but suddenly looks up to Taritie. "Are you certain? If you give me your word, I will commit myself to this."

By this point, Ashanna has stopped crying and rests in Taritie's arms. Using what strength she has, she pushes against him and stands by herself. "I know my parents believed in Taritie, and I do as well. I do not know if my father is alive or dead, but I know that he would tell me to build a new life here."

Taritie, seeing that it is decided, lets the others talk among themselves while he walks toward the entrance to the church. He takes another suspicious look at the capital, and under his breath, he mutters as if speaking to the city itself, "I do not doubt that while I build a new life here, you will not stop awakening. What other secrets have you been hiding?" He sighs and knows that he needs to focus on those he has sworn to protect. He does not need to worry about what cannot yet be seen.

www.ingramcontent.com/pod-product-compliance
Lightning Source LLC
Chambersburg PA
CBHW032124170626
46808CB00006B/2093